Tales From the Hereafter

ALSO BY TED MYERS

NOVELS
Fluffy's Revolution (2019)
Paris Escapade (2020)

MEMOIR
Making It: Music, Sex & Drugs
in the Golden Age of Rock (2017)

Tales From the Hereafter
by
Ted Myers

DEUXMERS

Published by Deuxmers, LLC
PO Box 440, Waimanalo, Hawaii.
deuxmers.com

Copyright © 2023 Ted Myers.
Cover design © Coşkun Çağlayan.
Author photograph © Janet Caliri.

"Bardo Train to Canarsie" originally published in *Literally Stories*, September 2016, and in *To Hull & Back Short Story Anthology 2016*, October 2016.
"For All Eternity" originally published in *One Hundred Voices*, vol. III, August 2017.
"Strangers on a Plane" originally published in *Bewildering Stories*, May 2018.
"The Waiting Room" originally published in *The Mystic Blue Review*, September 2017.
"I Dream in Black and White" originally published in *Ink Stains: A Dark Fiction Anthology*, vol. 9, July 2018.

The characters, names, businesses, places and incidents portrayed in this book are fictitious, and any resemblance to actual persons living or dead are purely coincidental.

All rights reserved. No part of this book may be reproduced, or stored in a retrieval system, or transmitted in any form or by any means, electronic, mechanical, photocopying, recording, or otherwise, without express written permission of the publisher, except for the use of brief quotations in a book review.

Printed in the United States of America.
ISBN: 978-1-944521-18-9 (Softcover)
ISBN: 978-1-944521-19-6 (Ebook)
First edition, August 2023

To my beloved Jaiananda.
See you on the other side?

CONTENTS

BOOK I

Introduction	1
Bardo Train to Canarsie	3
Powerless	10
The Book of Moments	15
Trainwreck	21
Strangers on a Plane	31
The Littlest Ghost	37
Betrayal	41
Shop Till You Drop	47
Possessed and Repossessed	59
Hell Hath No Fury	63
For All Eternity	74
Ghost Academy	77
Just Desserts	86
Monster Zoo	93
Perchance to Dream	97
Prisoners	101
The Waiting Room	105

BOOK II

Introduction	109
I Dream in Black and White	111

BOOK I

INTRODUCTION

Nearly everyone has some idea about what happens after you die. Most people get theirs from their religion. Most of the Western religions have some version of heaven and hell, and sometimes purgatory. The Buddhists and Hindus believe in reincarnation and karma. After some kind of in-between period, which the Tibetans call the *bardo*, we are reborn into a new body and live the life dictated by our karma. Our karma is the result of our actions in our previous life—how good or bad we were, or how much or little we evolved as humans. The idea is that every life has lessons for you to learn. If you don't learn the lessons that are given to you, you don't progress. Sometimes you regress. Once you've learned everything, you become an enlightened being and never have to occupy a physical body again. You become one with the Infinite, which is where we all came from in the first place. As you turn these pages, it will become clear to you that this belief system—the logic of it—makes the most sense to me, although most of my cosmologies are imagined.

The collection of stories in Book I consists of first-person accounts, direct from the afterlife. The fact that they vary wildly as to the way things work over there supports the basic premise that each person makes his or her own heaven or hell. Often, it isn't at all what they were expecting. One rule seems constant: We all ultimately get what we deserve.

Ted Myers
Santa Monica, June 2022

BARDO TRAIN TO CANARSIE

My body had been dead for two days. I could hear my brother monks chanting the mantra of the dead the whole time: "Go to the Light. Do not be distracted by the demons of the bardo…" If this was the bardo, it certainly was not what I was expecting.

I found myself on a swaying, rattling train that made its way at a frightening speed on screeching silver rails through tunnels that were beneath a huge, bustling city. Above the windows were rows of signs in English. They were advertisements of some kind, but I couldn't read them.

"Go to the Light," they said, so I made my way through sliding doors that separated the empty cars to the front car. I looked out the front window, and I did see a light. I was headed in the right direction! But it turned out to be just a station. The train stopped and the doors opened. I wondered if I should get off. A single passenger entered my car. He was a large man with wild hair and full beard. He was dressed in filthy rags and he carried an overpowering smell of urine.

"Hey, baby. Nice threads." he said, looking straight at me.

"Threads?"

"Yeah, man, your outfit. That's da *shit*. I wish I had me a rig like that."

I gathered he was referring to the burgundy and saffron robes I had worn all my life. The robes all the monks of my order wear every day. I never thought there was anything special about them, but seeing how impressed he was, I began to think maybe they were rather special, at least in contrast to him and these gray, dirty surroundings. The train pulled into another station. The doors opened again, but no one got on. My companion and I were still alone. In fact, there didn't seem to be any other passengers on the entire train.

I had no trouble understanding my companion's spoken English, even though the writing on the advertisements looked completely alien to me.

"How are you called?" I asked him.

"'Yo, muthafucka!'" He laughed loudly. Apparently he had made a joke, but I didn't get it.

"My dharma name is Dilgo Khyentse Rinpoche. I have many other names, though, some of them secret. You can call me Dilgo. Nice to meet you, Yo Muthafucka."

My companion had another hearty laugh. It was hard for him to stop laughing, but when he finally did, he said, as straight-faced as he could, "Nice to meet you, Dildo!"

"It's Dilgo."

"Yeah, I know. I was just playin' wit' cha. By the way, my name is Leroy. Leroy C.V. Jones, writer, poet extraordinaire and bon vivant, at your service."

I looked at him in puzzlement.

"Just call me Leroy. Say, you a monk, right?"

"Yes."

"From Tibet?"

I brightened. This man knew more than he let on. "Actually, Nepal. We were all driven out of our home, Tibet, many years ago. In 1959."

"1959? What year is it now, anyway?"

"In Western time, the year is 2020."

"No. You're shittin' me!"

"I shit you not."

"I been dead since 1965."

The train stopped again. "Union Square," said Leroy. "Let's get off and change to the Broadway line. Maybe we can catch Bird."

"Bird?"

"Charlie Parker, man. You never heard of Charlie Parker?"

"No."

"Only the greatest saxophone player that ever lived. The greatest *musician* that ever lived. Sometimes he plays on the 49th Street platform. If we're lucky, we can catch him. It is absolutely the best thing about being dead… Hey, listen to this…"

He positioned his hands as if playing an invisible saxophone and sang a fast and complex series of notes. These notes had a certain universal truth to them, so that, as alien as this music was, it communicated something to me.

"That was called 'Au Privave,' a Charlie Parker tune. Great, huh?"

"Yes, great."

He stuck his hand out to keep the doors from closing. "You sure you don't wanna go to 49th Street with me?"

"No, I think it is better for me to stay on this bardo train. I must go toward the Light." I gestured toward the front window. Leroy let the doors close and looked out at the tunnel ahead.

"I don't see no light. I see a lotta lights—red ones, green ones, white ones…"

"Well, I do see a light, and I'm going to it."

"Okay, brotha-man, I'll go to da Light wit' cha."

"Can I trust you?"

"Now, what kinda crazy-ass question is that? If you couldn't trust me, I'd tell you you could trust me. If you could trust me, I'd tell you you could trust me. So, you believe what you want."

"In our *Book of the Dead*, it warns us to beware of demons who will distract you and draw you away from the Light. Are you one of those?"

"Not that I know of, man. But I've been called worse."

The train stopped at First Avenue; no one got on. We then descended into a long, black tunnel. I sensed we were under a body of water.

"Is there water above us?" I asked him.

"Yeah, the East River. Soon we'll be in Brooklyn."

"What is in Brooklyn?"

"Nothin', man. Usually I just stay on the train when it gets to Canarsie and go back the other way. When we get back to Manhattan, I'm goin' to 49th Street. You can come with or not. Your choice. One thing I can tell ya: there ain't shit in Canarsie."

At the first stop in Brooklyn a group of six young men entered our car. They looked at us, whispered together and laughed. The largest one approached us.

"What the fuck you doin' on our train?" he asked. His voice had a belligerent tone.

Leroy responded defiantly: "What choo mean 'our train'? This here's a public conveyance."

The leader approached Leroy, sniffed him. "Man, you stink like a toilet! Hey," he beckoned to the others in his group, "come here and smell this guy."

"Pee-yooo," they all said, holding their noses.

"And look at this one," said another, fingering my robes in a most disrespectful manner. "What are you dressed up for? Is it Halloween already?"

"I do not know of this Halloween," I said. They all laughed. These youths were definitely threatening us. I felt that they were working themselves up for a physical attack. But, if we—Leroy and I—were already dead, what could they do to us?

The youth that had addressed me turned to the others. "He don't know about Halloween! Hey, where the fuck you from, anyway, China?"

"Nepal," I said.

"Never heard of it. Must be one of those piddly-ass countries over in Asia."

"That is correct," I said.

The train pulled into another station and stopped.

"Let's throw them off the train," said the leader. "Man, you in Crip territory here. You won't last five minutes."

"No. I must stay on this bardo train."

They all started to grab me. Leroy ran to the other end of the car and cowered behind a seat. Instinctively, I defended myself, using the ancient Tibetan martial art of Sengueï Ngaro. In a flash, all six men were scattered on the floor of the train. The doors of the car were still open and all of them got up and fled as the doors closed. The bardo train moved on toward the Light.

Leroy got up from the floor behind the seat where he had been hiding. "Holy shit, Dilgo, you kicked their asses! My *man*!"

"They forced me to break my vow of nonviolence. I wonder if this will affect my karma adversely in my next incarnation."

"You be alright," said Leroy. "None of them was hurt so bad they couldn't get up and run."

"You speak wisely, Leroy." His words comforted me. "I think perhaps these were the demons the Book warns of. How did you die, Leroy?"

"I was livin' on the streets. It was a very cold night. I got drunk on some cheap wine and fell asleep in a doorway. And I woke up here."

"Sounds like a good death," I said.

"It was! A very good death. I never felt a thing. Hell, I'd pick that death over some kinda cancer any day of the week. How did you die, Dilgo?"

"I lived 101 years on earth. Peacefully, happily. Then I got very tired, so I left my body."

"Wow. Now that sounds like a *great* death."

"Yes, it was. All my brother monks were around me, chanting me into the next stage of existence. But I must admit, I never expected this. What do you do here?"

"I just ride different subways from station to station. I take the A train, the double E, the IRT, this used to be the BMT. Of course, they don't call them that anymore, but I'm still in 1965."

"Do you ever get out of the subway?"

"Never. I can never get upstairs to the surface. And the only other people I see are dead like me."

"Then those boys, the ones I beat up, they must be dead too."

"Damn right. They be dead as mackerels. They just ain't figured that out yet. And the station where they ran away, Lorimer Street... They were right, that is Crip territory, but it's dead Crip territory. Of all the stations in the subway system, Lorimer Street is the closest to hell. The Crips there make you watch as they kill and mutilate everyone you've ever loved or cared about. I made the mistake of getting off there once, but I was lucky. I managed to cross to the other platform and get on the train goin' the other way before they got finished killing my mother."

I was looking out the front window as we neared the next stop. It was the next-to-last stop on the line, the one before Canarsie. "Look, Leroy! Can you see the Light? It's getting brighter now."

"Yeah. It is getting brighter. I can see it, Dilgo!"

The train stopped at East 105th Street and Turnbull Avenue. The doors opened and a monster got on our car. He looked and smelled like a rotting corpse. He walked stiffly, like a reanimated dead person. When he tried to speak, guttural, gurgling sounds came out of his mouth. He approached us with outstretched arms, gurgling.

"Ahhh! What's that, Dilgo? Let's get the hell out of here!" Leroy started to run for the exit while the doors were still open. I grabbed him and held him back.

"No. This is another trick of the bardo to keep us from the Light. This creature is here to test our courage. Stand still and don't move. It cannot hurt us."

"Its stink is already hurtin' me," said Leroy.

"Just stay still. Only one more stop to go."

The white Light of Canarsie filled our car as we rolled into the Rockaway Parkway station. It was almost too bright to see the details of the station, but I could see there were stairs that led up from the platform.

"Goddamn. I wish I had my shades. I left them on a train about twenty years ago," said Leroy.

"Don't worry, Leroy. You will soon get used to the brightness."

As we rolled into the station, the creature dissolved into the Light. The train stopped, the doors opened, and we walked out onto the platform.

"Where we goin?" asked Leroy. His voice quivered with trepidation. "I don't wanna go to Canarsie."

"It is not Canarsie, Leroy. It is the next phase of our existence." I led him up the stairs. Sweet-smelling air was wafting in from above.

"But I can't go like this," he said. "Look at my…" He looked down at his clothes to see his rags were gone and he was now resplendent in a beautifully-tailored white silk suit with matching white buck shoes. "Look at my clothes! These are the baddest, most splendiferous mutha-fuckin' threads of all time!"

"Yes," I said, "and you smell good, too."

POWERLESS

It's no fun being murdered. Try raped and murdered. Try having your throat slit, feeling the life blood spill out of you, knowing all the time what's happening to you, and being powerless to stop it. That's what happened to me. You wouldn't like it.

They say you can't make it into heaven with anger in your heart. And so I hung around here, neither angel nor devil, just a sixteen-year-old ghost, craving revenge. Do you know what it's like being a ghost? Of course you don't, because you're reading this book. If you were a ghost, you couldn't even pick it up. You couldn't turn a page. You can see and hear everything that's happening in the world, but you can't do a thing. It's like you're made of air.

Most ghosts hang around their bodies, but my killer chopped mine up and burned it in a furnace in the basement of the old school, so I hung around him. I'd watch and I'd wait. I'd wait for a chance, some way to trip him up.

My name was Mary Beth Caruthers. Now I have no name because no one can see or hear me. My family is poor. They live in Lodenville, Georgia, a very small town. Sometimes I'd visit my mother and two brothers, but they didn't know I was there.

They didn't know I was murdered, only disappeared. The cops gave up looking for me after a few weeks. My mother was very sad all the time. My younger brother, Petey, he's five, acted like he'd already forgotten me, always horsing around and laughing and fighting. There was a picture of me tacked to the wall of their room, a "missing" poster. For a while, they were tacked up all over town, but then most of them came down or were blown away. My older brother, Jimmy John, he's twelve. He looked at it a lot. I knew he was thinking of me.

We're what people call poor white trash. But we're not trash. My daddy was. He left us right after Petey was born. But my mama is a good Christian woman. She took us to church every Sunday and she taught us the difference between right and wrong. She works the night shift at the In-N-Out Burger and then a day shift at the Walmart. She won't go on welfare.

Mostly I'd hang around my school, Lodenville High School. In the basement where Bob burned up my body. Bob Pritchett is my killer. He worked as the school janitor. He was white trash too. And a drifter. I was afraid he would move on to some other town soon and murder some other young girl. It's what he did. I tried to figure out how to get him before he did.

Bob usually lived in his car, but in winter, on cold nights, he stayed in the school basement and got the big old furnace going good and hot so he could keep warm. He drank a lot, cheap whiskey or wine, and then pass out on the boiler room floor.

One night, I was in there watching him sleep when an angel came to me. Well, maybe she wasn't a real angel. She looked like just a girl about my age. She wore a Catholic girls' school uniform and she had a scar across her neck just like mine.

"You must let go of your hate for him," she said, looking at Bob. "You want to get into heaven, don't you?"

"Sure," I said, "but if you think it's so easy, you try getting raped and your throat slit."

"I did. By him," she said.

I was amazed. "Well, how did you do it? How did you stop hating him?"

"I prayed for guidance, and an angel came to me and said 'Your hate will not hurt him, it will only hurt you. Have faith. Everyone gets what they deserve, including him. Only God can say when.' Night after night, day after day, I prayed to be free of my hate. I pictured that angel in my mind. And at last, I looked into my heart and found no more hate. That's when I ascended."

"Well, how did you come back here?"

"I had to get special permission to come back to help you because we all could see how you were suffering."

I thought long and hard about that. I wanted to get into heaven—whatever that was—sure. But I was very attached to my hatred of Bob and I wanted to be the one to bring him to his just reward. I guess it's the nature of people. Someone does a bad thing to us, or our mother, or our brother, and we get so mad, we think it will make us feel better to get the person who did the bad thing. But now I was starting to think it wouldn't make me feel any better if I could kill Bob with my bare hands. Would it bring me back, alive and whole, to my family? I thought on it and I prayed on it.

*

Late one night, I tried an experiment. I went to my brothers' room and I whispered in the ear of Jimmy John, who was fast asleep and dreaming. "Jimmy John," I said, "Bob Pritchett killed me. Don't try to hurt him. But find some evidence to send him to prison. Look in the school furnace. That's where he burned my body."

The next morning, Jimmy John woke up and told Petey of the strange dream he had. "I dreamed Mary Beth came to me and told me Bob Pritchett killed her."

"Aww, you're crazy," said Petey.

Jimmy John didn't say anything, but he couldn't get the dream out of his head. He took to following Bob around, watching him as much as he could.

The school was an old building and, on the alley side, it had small windows along the base of one wall that looked into the boiler room. One Saturday when the school was closed, Jimmy John got into the basement through one of the windows. He pried it open with a screwdriver. He brought with him a small gardening spade. He went to the furnace, which was turned off, and poked around in the ashes. Way in the back, and buried deep in the ash, he felt something hard. He scooped it out. It was a fragment of bone. My bone.

I yelled in Jimmy John's ear: "Take it to the police, Jimmy John." But Jimmy John didn't hear me. Being human like me, he was now bent on taking his own revenge.

Monday night was especially cold. Jimmy John sneaked out of the house and went over to the school. He looked in the window and could see Bob, by the light of the roaring fire in the furnace, drinking and staggering around in there. I was in there with him, but Jimmy John couldn't see me. Bob was yelling at some invisible people and waving his bottle of whiskey around. He did this often. Finally, he hurled the bottle into the furnace. The fire in the furnace flared up.

That's what gave Jimmy John the idea. He went home and got a gasoline can. He took it to the local gas station and had the man fill it up with gas. He found an empty whiskey bottle and a rag. He soaked the rag in gasoline, filled the bottle, stuffed the rag in the mouth of the bottle, grabbed some matches, and went back to the school.

I could see what Jimmy John meant to do. I flew out one of the basement windows and yelled in his ear: "Don't do it, Jimmy John! I don't hate him anymore. He's suffering more alive than he would dead." But Jimmy John couldn't hear me. First, he grabbed a big rock and threw it through the window. Bob turned around and yelled, "Who did that?" He staggered over to the broken window and peered out. Jimmy John looked him straight in the eye and said: "This is for my sister." He lit the rag on fire and threw the bottle through the window.

The fire from the explosion burnt Bob to a crisp, but it also came shooting out the basement window and burnt Jimmy John real bad. He was taken to the hospital. He suffered a long time before he died.

※

The three of us haunted the basement of the new school, the one they built after the old one burnt down. Bob, Jimmy John, and me. We could all see and hear each other, but no one could see or hear us, and we soon ran out of stuff to talk about. I figured we were trapped there together forever, powerless, that this would be our hell. But then, one day, the Catholic school girl appeared again.

"Mary Beth, you and Jimmy John are being lifted up. Come with me." She took me by the hand and I held Jimmy John's hand, and we ascended.

"Hey, where you goin'?" said Bob.

The Catholic school angel turned to him. "You'd do better to ask where *you're* going."

THE BOOK OF MOMENTS

I awoke in a dark, misty place. I could make out a few leafless, forlorn trees—a petrified forest—but nothing else. Nothing, that is, except a gigantic leatherbound book that lay at my feet. On the cover, in gilt letters, were my name and two dates: my birthday and today.

"Open the book," said a deep commanding voice.
"Where am I?"
"You are in the Preliminary Zone."
"Preliminary to what?"
"Preliminary to the In Between."

It started to dawn on me that I was dead. I was alive when I went to sleep last night, and now I wasn't. "Am I dead?" I asked the disembodied voice.

"You are. Open the book."
"What will happen if I do?"

"Each page represents a high point in your life. They are in chronological order. You will be in that time and place, re-living that moment. Choose the moment you would like to stay in for your period of In Between and you will stay there until it is time for you to go into a new body."

"How long will that be?"

"It's different for each person. Time is not the same here, but, if you must have a number, it will be equivalent to 300 years. Open the book and choose."

"Can I review all the choices before I make my decision?"

"No. When you get to the right one, you will know it and not want to go on."

I open the book.

*

I'm two. I'm in my Grandma Ella's arms. Her old skin is wrinkly, soft, squishy, welcoming. We are in her bedroom, which used to be the parlor before my father (her son) and his pregnant wife moved in with her after the War. There was a big housing shortage in 1945 because of all those GIs coming home with wives and new babies.

We sat in a chair and looked out the window on Topping Avenue in the Bronx. It's a quiet street in a quiet, middle-class neighborhood. Parked cars line both sides of the street. "Car," I say, pointing out the window.

"Yes, darling, those are cars. You are very smart."

I know my Grandma Ella loves me more than anyone else in the world. Her husband, who I was named for, died a year before I was born, and she needed something to fill the hole in that big, warm heart of hers. So I was it. But it went beyond that, the bond between me and Grandma Ella. We each loved the other more than anyone else. I loved my parents too, but not like Grandma Ella. She loved me more than either of her two sons, and I loved her more than either of my parents. My mother didn't like hugging and snuggling very much. She didn't know how to demonstrate affection very well. My father was better at it, but he was more in his head, less in his heart.

It would not be a bad place to spend a few hundred years, here in the arms of Grandma Ella, engulfed in unconditional love. Maybe I should stop right here. Does it get any better? I leafed through the pages of my life in my head. This had to be close to as good as it got. But there was someplace else I wanted to go back to. Someplace twenty-three years further on. It was less certain. There was more risk, but my desire outweighed my trepidation and I turned the page, saying a tearful goodbye to Grandma Ella.

※

I'm eight. My dad and I are on a nature walk in the wooded countryside of Duchess County, New York. It's Summer and, since my parents are both teachers, we all get to go to the country together for the entire summer. My dad knows all the different kinds of trees and bushes, weeds and flowers. We spot little animals, squirrels, and rabbits. A raccoon. A skunk. We find a baby bird that's fallen out of its nest, but the nest it too high for us to put it back. "Besides," says my father, "if the mother smells people on her baby, she will not feed it and let it die. It's better to let it die naturally. Some animal will probably eat it."

"No!" I protested in tears. "Let's take it home and raise it ourselves."

"We couldn't take care of it, son. Death is part of life. Although it may seem cruel to us, it's the way things were meant to be."

We came upon some crabapple trees and we picked and ate some sour green apples. They were sour in a good way. That was the closest I ever felt to my father and it was one of the best days of my life. But, still, I knew I needed to move on.

I turned the page.

※

I'm ten. I have a mad crush on a girl in my fifth-grade class, Judy Sonnenheim. There's just been a blizzard and school is closed. Snow is still falling lightly. It covers everything in my neighborhood in pristine whiteness. The snow plows have cleared the street, burying the cars up to the door handles.

The other kids are all having snowball wars, hiding behind walls of plowed snow, but I walk to Judy's building and just wait. I look up at her fourth-floor window and wonder if she'll come out. I'm bundled up in my heavy sweater, winter coat, mittens, and hat with earflaps, but still, I'm freezing. At last, she comes out. She smiles at me. I act surprised to bump into her (right in front of her building). She asks me if I want to make snow angels. I look around to make sure none of my friends are watching. Then, we lie on our backs in a virgin plot of snow and flap our arms and legs, making snow angels. Sometimes our hands or legs brush against each other. I'm in heaven.

But I turn the page.

*

I'm thirteen. I've been taking guitar lessons. My parents have just bought me my first electric guitar, and I love it. I've discovered I have a good ear, a good singing voice, and a talent for figuring out the chord changes of songs I hear on the radio. The year is 1959. My friend Johnny has also started playing guitar and sings pretty well. We decide to work up a couple of songs for the school talent show. We are in eighth grade. We decide on "Dream" by the Everly Brothers and "That'll Be the Day" by Buddy Holly. So, we start practicing, and we discover we have a good vocal blend. Johnny plays acoustic guitar and I play electric. I learn the lead guitar part on "That'll Be the Day," and pretty well nail it. I sound just like Buddy Holly. By the time the day of the show rolls around, we are sounding very tight. Most of the other kids just get up and sing along with records. Then it's our turn. I look out over the auditorium. It's filled with the expectant faces of just about everyone I know. When Johnny and I cut loose with "That'll Be the Day," the place goes wild. That feeling of adoration from a big crowd is the strongest kick I've ever felt. It's addictive, and it makes me decide: this is what I want to do for the rest of my life. After "Dream," they cheer even louder. We win the talent contest by a mile, and my career as a rock musician is launched.

That was certainly one of the very highest moments of my life, but—I turn the page.

*

I'm nineteen. I'm onstage in front of the largest audience we've ever played for—maybe 5,000 people, all screaming their heads off. My first band has just been signed by Capitol Records—the label of two of my idols: The Beatles and The Beach Boys. We are opening for The Beach Boys on the East Coast leg of their national tour. I've been writing some catchy original songs, and they are going over big with the fans. I feel like a real rock star. Although it was short-lived, that glory moment in my long career as a musician was certainly a high point. Should I stay here? No. I know where I want to go. I turn the page...

*

This is it. I'm twenty-five. I'm in bed with Rebecca, the first woman I've ever been truly in love with. I've had lots of experience with sex, and a lot of things I thought were love, but this is different. This is the real thing. We are like two parts of a single thing. When I enter her, the circuit is completed, and we become one. We become lost in each other. This is the moment I want to stay in forever. The only trouble is, she is married. Married to a rich and powerful man. A dangerous man. They don't live together, but this is his house. He thinks of her as his property. He can come and go, unannounced, as he pleases. We never know when he might show up. And, more than once, I've found myself fleeing out the back door as he was walking in the front. We fall asleep.

*

And I wake up here, in this strange landscape.

"This is where I want to stop," I tell the voice.

"That's just as well because this was your final choice."

"It was?"

"Yes."

"Fine," I say.

"Then, so be it. You will be able to make love to Rebecca for the next 300 years. Would you like to see what happens next?"

"Okay," I say. And a strange feeling of foreboding comes over me.

Suddenly, the perspective changes. I can see Rebecca and me asleep in bed together. Her husband walks in quietly. He takes a pillow and smothers her to death. Then he does the same to me.

"So we both died that night? Last night?"

"Yes," says the voice.

"Then why isn't she here with me?"

"I am."

I turn, and Rebecca is right there behind me. We embrace. Then we are back in her bedroom, on the bed, making love. Forever.

TRAINWRECK

Through the smoke and flames, I could see a few others wandering around in a daze. The bodies of the dead and wounded were strewn amidst the twisted wreckage of the Acela Express; the 1:15 from Grand Central to Boston, which had derailed for no apparent reason. But, as we rounded that last curve, I had seen a man in a black watch cap doing something on the tracks up ahead. Then he ran to a nearby SUV, got in, and waited. Then everything went black. I never heard the explosion.

Sirens were approaching from all directions. Soon the firemen and EMTs arrived and began pulling the bodies out of the wreckage and placing the wounded on stretchers, which were hustled into ambulances and medivac helicopters. The dead were left for last. Among the last remaining bodies, pinned beneath a large piece of train, I saw myself. A large glass shard had nearly split me in two at the sternum. At last, they extricated my body and loaded it onto a stretcher. They covered my face with a sheet. They did the same with five other people, two men and three women. I looked at their faces and realized they were the same five people that had been stumbling around with me and were now standing beside me, solemn and bewildered, looking down at their sheet-covered bodies, all in a row. We turned and looked at each other.

I'm a writer, or at least I was. I wrote mysteries and thrillers, and I'd trained myself to observe. Maybe that's why I saw what no one else did. No one who survived, that is.

"Looks like we're dead," I remarked to no one in particular.

"I can't be dead," said a young woman in tears. "I have a small child at home."

"I have a major business deal to finalize," said a middle-aged man in a suit.

"Call your secretary and have her cancel all your appointments," I said, with a smile. I offered him my cell phone.

"Oh, you're a laugh riot," said the man. He didn't appreciate my humor. But few did.

"My heart goes out to you young people," chimed in an old woman. She was probably in her early seventies, with long white hair done up in a single braid down her back. She was dressed in an Indian kurta and flowing yoga pants. "Being dead doesn't feel bad to me at all. In fact, I feel better than I have in a long time. But, then, I've lived a long, full life. I can't wait to see what comes next."

"Now my damn husband will get all my money," said the third woman, a middle-aged brunette, attractive in a brittle way. "I was on my way to sign the divorce papers. Now the bastard gets everything by default."

"Do you really care?" I said. "I mean, 'you can't take it with you,' right?"

"That's not the point. I just wanted him to suffer. Now he'll be laughing at my grave."

"I want to see my baby," the young woman wailed. "I have to go." She turned and walked off in a northerly direction, following the railroad tracks.

"Hey wait!" I called after her. I ran to catch up with her, but it was more like — zip — I was suddenly right beside her. "I think, if you close your eyes and picture your home and your baby, you'll get there faster." I have no idea where I got this notion, and I was sure I was talking through my ass, but the next second, she was gone. Disappeared.

"Hey, did you see that?" I asked the others. They all nodded, wide-eyed. "Let's all go see her baby," I said enthusiastically. "All we have to do is close our eyes and picture that girl at home with her baby, and we'll be there."

"You could be right, young man," said the old woman, "but don't you think it might be a bit inappropriate for us all to show up at a moment like this?"

"Oh... Yeah, I guess you're right. I got a little carried away with my new powers. But think of it: we could will ourselves to go anywhere right now."

"The only place I want to go is up," said the old woman, pointing skyward.

"She's right," said the businessman. "The only thing to do when you die is go to heaven."

"Or the other place," I said, smiling, giving a thumbs-down. Suits always rub me the wrong way, and vice-versa.

"Boy, you're a real wet blanket, aren't you, kid?"

"Sorry, mister. No offense intended. But you don't really believe in that heaven and hell stuff, do you?"

"I most certainly do," said the man.

"I believe in reincarnation," said the old lady.

"What about you, lady?" I asked the brittle brunette.

"I don't know. I never really thought about it much. But I know what I'd like to do."

"What?" we all asked in unison.

"I'd like to haunt that rotten husband of mine, and his new girlfriend."

"I want to go to heaven," said the businessman, "but first, I want to attend my own funeral. I want to see how many people show up. Everybody who's anybody, I'll bet."

"Careful. 'Pride goeth before a fall,'" said the old lady.

"What makes any of you think we have any choice in the matter?" asked the brittle brunette.

"She's right," I said. "I think all we have to do now is sit and wait for something to happen. But do we have to do it standing over our mangled bodies? Why don't we sit under that tree?" I indicated a majestic oak nearby.

"I read somewhere that the Tibetans believe the soul should not linger near the body, or risk remaining on earth as a ghost for all time," said the old lady.

"Yeah," I said. "I read some stuff like that too."

We drifted over to the tree and sat down. Now I could see state troopers clearing and sifting through the debris. A forensics team was supervising. They examined the sections of track that had been blown sky-high. I knew they would soon learn what I already knew.

Until now, the sixth man, the engineer, had remained ruefully silent. He was a Black man in his mid-fifties. He wore the standard Amtrak engineer uniform: navy blue cap and pants, white shirt, red tie.

"It was all my fault," he said, hanging his head "I saw somebody on the tracks up ahead. If only I could've stopped fast enough, but we were going so fast…"

"I saw him too," I said. "It wasn't your fault. Nobody could've stopped the train that fast. It was sabotage, no doubt about it."

"My God! Terrorists!" said the businessman. "We have to tell them somehow."

"Oh, they'll know soon enough," I said. "But we need to tell them what we saw." I turned to the engineer. "Did you see his car?"

"No. I was too busy trying to stop the train."

"I did. It was a gray SUV. A Nissan, I think. I wonder if anyone can see or hear us?"

"I doubt it. I mean, let's face it, we're ghosts…" said the brittle brunette.

"Damn! I'd love to help with that investigation," I said. "This is right down my alley."

"Did you say you were some sort of writer?" asked the old lady.

"Yeah. I write mysteries and thrillers... Hey, wait a minute. I never said anything about that to any of you."

"Oh," said the old lady somewhat absently. "I guess I just picked it up."

"Picked it up?"

"Yes. I'm a psychic, you see."

"Something's happening to me," said the brunette. She became incandescent, glowing with a golden light. "Oh... Oh, it's, it's wonderful!"

Then, poof! She was gone.

"Yeah, me too," said the businessman. "Uh-oh. Oh no, oh no!" He took on a dark aura, and then he, too, disappeared. Where they went, we can only speculate. Now it was just me, the engineer, and the old lady.

"What now, psychic lady?"

"My name's Beth."

"Oh. Sorry, Beth. Mine's James."

"Mine's Chester," said the engineer. There followed a long, pensive silence.

"Why them and not us?" I said at last.

"Only a guess, but I'd say we were 'detained' for a reason," said Beth.

"To help catch the terrorist," I said excitedly.

"You said 'terrorist'," said Beth. "Does that mean you think it was one man acting alone?"

"Yes," I said, "but don't ask me why. If you can pick up on people's thoughts, can you also transmit thoughts to others?"

"Sometimes. But they have to be a bit psychic too."

"Let's go over there and whisper in their ears. Maybe one of them will hear."

A helicopter landed and an FBI team of three men emerged and consulted briefly with the head of the forensics team.

The forensics team consisted of two men and two women.

By now, all the wounded had been taken to hospitals and the state police had cordoned off the area with wooden barricades and yellow crime scene tape. Now the only people allowed among the wreckage were the four forensics experts, who wore surgical gloves and laminated white tags around their necks.

"Try the women first," I whispered to Beth. "They seem to be more receptive than men."

"Why are you whispering?" Beth smiled. "Afraid they'll hear us?"

"Au contraire," I said. Then I yelled. "Hey, any of you guys hear us?" No one reacted.

I drifted over to the place where the bomb had been planted. Beside the blast hole where the track used to be, there was a cigarette butt — and a footprint in the muddy soil, facing away, toward the road. By the size of the crater, I guessed it had been a relatively small explosion. Just enough to take out a few feet of rail. "Look at this," I said to Beth. "I can't believe none of them has found this."

"I'll try steering that woman over here," said Beth. She was looking at a young, attractive woman with auburn hair. *Mmmm, not bad,* I thought, *too bad I'm dead.* Beth went over and whispered in her ear. And, sure enough, she turned and headed over to where I was standing. Her ID tag read: Charlotte Sawyer, Department of Homeland Security.

"Hi, Charlotte," I said, not really expecting a reaction. "Look at the ground."

Amazingly, she looked down, saw the cigarette butt and then the footprint.

"Hey!" She called to the others, "George, Jack, Maria. I found something."

Her colleagues all came over, treading carefully, so as not to contaminate any evidence. George, who seemed to be in command, said, "Jack, take some pictures." Jack took several photos of the blast hole, and then the butt and its proximity to the footprint. George picked up the butt with tweezers and dropped it into a small plastic bag. Then Jack took more photos of the footprint from various angles and real close. He took out a tape measure and measured the footprint, then photographed the print with the tape measure. He did this with both the length and the width of the print.

"Size 8½ D, I'd say," said Jack.

"There are traces of gunpowder in the hole," said George, who had been gently poking around the blast hole with a small spoon. He took a sample and put it in another plastic bag.

"Gunpowder," I said to Beth and Chester. "Not C-4. Nothing sophisticated. Looks like a real amateur job. I don't think this is the work of an Islamic terrorist organization. Not their style. They could have blown the whole train to smithereens, killed everyone. This guy just wanted to derail it."

"Makes sense," said Chester. "Of course, I don't know diddly squat about these things. But it sounds like you do."

"I've done a lot of research for my writing. Beth, do you think you can get what I just said across to Charlotte?"

"I'll try."

Beth tried, and it worked.

Charlotte stood over the small blast hole. "Hey," she shouted to the others. "I don't think it was a terrorist organization. Too amateurish. Gunpowder? Who uses gunpowder? And this guy just used enough to blow up the one rail. Real terrorists would have planted charges all up and down the line to kill as many people as they could. I think he's homegrown. And, what's more, I think he lives nearby."

She thought of that last part by herself. And it made sense. Some nut living in isolation in rural Connecticut that hates the railroad for some reason. A disgruntled employee?

"Tell her he drives a gray SUV—a Nissan I think," I told Beth.

She relayed the message. By now Charlotte had gotten the puzzled attention of the other three forensics people.

"Okay. Now you're really gonna think I'm nuts..."

"Yeah?" said the others in unison.

"I think he drives a gray Nissan SUV."

"Now, where in the hell did you get that?" asked Jack.

"I can't say for sure... but it feels like somebody's whispering in my ear."

"My old Mexican *abuela* used to hear voices," offered Maria, "and they were usually right."

"What the hell," said George. "Let's have the FBI guys run a check on all gray Nissan SUVs in a fifty-mile radius. What could it hurt? And, besides, we haven't got anything else to go on."

It didn't take the FBI long to run the check. It immediately came up with only fourteen candidates. And one of them was registered to a certain Rupert Helms, formerly an engineer for Amtrak. Fired for being drunk on the job. A background check also revealed he had ties to a white supremacist organization called Arian America. His replacement was Chester, a Black man. There it was: motive, method, and opportunity. His address was less than forty miles away.

"Let's go see this Rupert Helms," said Agent Poltorak, the chief FBI officer.

The FBI guys only had the helicopter, and the forensics team had a Chevy Tahoe. It was decided that arriving in the helicopter would give the guy too much warning, so we all piled into the Tahoe. It was a huge vehicle, so plenty of room, especially since three of us were ghosts. Beth, Chester, and I got into the way-back. You could have installed a jacuzzi in there. I really wanted to sit next to Charlotte, who was sending out heavy attraction vibes to me (although I knew this was impossible, since she didn't know I existed), but I contented myself with leaning up against the back side of the seat in which she was sitting, putting the back of my head against hers, and smelling her hair, which was like an aphrodisiac to me.

Of course, the state police wanted in, so Poltorak grudgingly agreed that they should follow us to the address. On the way, Poltorak radioed headquarters on the status of the investigation and let them know we were headed to Helms' address to interrogate and, in all probability, make the arrest.

We headed about twenty miles north on I-95, then turned inland somewhere north of New London. The roads got smaller and smaller, and finally, we found ourselves on a narrow two-lane blacktop. It was beginning to get dark. We finally came to a mailbox that said Helms, and made a right onto a dirt road that led to a ramshackle cabin deep in the woods. We turned out our lights for the last hundred yards, but it was no use. As soon as we got out of the car, a blinding bank of floodlights that were mounted on the roof came on, and we found ourselves pinned down by automatic rifle fire. All of the living dove for cover behind the nearest log or fence. The three of us dead people didn't bother. Poltorak got on the bullhorn.

"Helms. Rupert Helms. This is the FBI. You are surrounded. Come out with your hands over your head. You have thirty seconds."

Meanwhile, the state cops fanned out, crouching low in the darkness, trying to actually surround the house. Helms was a good shot. He picked off one of the staties, who, fortunately, was not seriously wounded. The FBI and all the cops returned a barrage of fire. All the windows of the cabin were shattered and the walls were riddled with bullet holes.

Finally, Helms yelled, "All right. I'm comin' out."

The door opened. Charlotte stood up to capture the moment with her phone camera. Helms emerged, gun in hand. He took one last shot. It hit Charlotte squarely in the chest. Then he was shot to pieces by the police. We saw his soul escape from his body. It was a shriveled, black thing, the color of gunpowder. We heard it scream and then explode in a burst of black smoke.

It was too late to save Charlotte. Everyone converged on her lifeless body. A state police medic frantically tried to resuscitate her, but it was no use. We stood around her, Beth, Chester, and I, and saw her soul emerge from her body, radiant. She came toward me. She was smiling. She drifted right up to me, looked me right in the eye. I smiled back.

"So this is death," she said. "Not so bad."

STRANGERS ON A PLANE

We were seated next to each other, two young men in their twenties, flying from New York to Los Angeles. I'm not a bad looking chap, but this guy was a knockout. There was an immediate attraction. The way he looked at me, I could tell there was chemistry for him too. He struck up the conversation and somehow got my whole story, albeit a false one. He told me his name was Rod — Rodney French to his future fans.

"You flying on business?" he asked.

"In a way. I came into some money — a lot of money — and I have to see a lawyer in LA to claim it."

"No kidding. Congratulations! Was it a close relative?"

"Actually, it's someone I've never even met. A great uncle or something. It seems I'm his only living relative."

"You said a lot of money. Mind telling me how much?"

"Fourteen million dollars." I don't know why I told him this. I can see now it was a mistake.

He whistled softly. "You're a lucky man."

"How about you. Why're you going to LA?"

"Oh... I've been offered a small part in a movie. I act."

"Wow, that's exciting. I wish I was creative."

"Acting's not that hard — it's just lying with style, pretending you're something you're not. I was in a play off-Broadway and some Hollywood producer spotted me, offered me a part — well, it's not in the bag yet. I have to do a screen test."

We discovered we were both twenty-seven. We were just about the same height and weight. We looked a lot alike, except that he had fair hair and mine was dark. I had a slight bump on my nose; his was straight. We could have been brothers. It came out that he had spent his last dime on the plane fare. He was betting the farm on that screen test.

"I guess I'll sleep in the airport and then try to bum a ride to Burbank. That's where the film company is."

"Don't be silly," I said. "I've reserved a suite at the Beverly Hilton. You can stay with me."

"Really? That's so kind of you. Thanks!"

"It'll be a pleasure," I said, raising one eyebrow to punctuate the innuendo.

That night, in the Beverly Hilton, we made love with abandon. Then Rodney smothered me to death with a pillow as I slept. I woke up in time to realize I was being murdered, but too late to do anything about it. I know he intended to take all the papers relating to my inheritance, my passport, my driver's license, dye his hair to match mine, and give himself the little bump in the nose with his actor's makeup kit.

But, of course, he found no such papers because I had lied about the inheritance. Instead, he found in my suitcase the $14 million in negotiable bonds I had stolen from my employer, Hereford Stanley, an investment bank in New York. How I got my hands on those bonds and to whom they belonged is a long and twisted tale. Suffice it to say that my scheme was complex and sophisticated enough for me to avoid detection, but only for a day or two. Just enough time for me to unload the bonds to a contact I had at a shady Philippine bank in LA, collect the cash—less his commission of $1 million—get phony ID documents made, drop off the cash with my accomplice, and grab a plane to Thailand. My ultimate destination was an obscure little beach where there were many American ex-pats. More than a few were fugitives of justice like myself. I was crazy about Rodney. I would have gladly taken him along, if only he hadn't killed me.

But now Rodney was stuck in the Beverly Hilton with my dead body and a bundle of hot bonds and no idea what to do with them. He didn't know about my guy at the bank.

*

After my soul left my body, it did not ascend to heaven or plunge to the fiery depths of hell. I never believed in any of that stuff anyway. No, I stayed right there with Rodney, right in the hotel suite. I wanted to see what would happen next. I could almost read all the questions racing through his mind: *How will I dispose of the body? Should I take his identity? These bonds say "negotiable," but how?*

I watched as he counted the bonds. They were each worth $10,000. "Fourteen million, just like he said," he muttered to himself. "He must've stolen them. I'm sittin' on fourteen million in negotiable bonds, but how do I unload them?" He paced the room, thinking, thinking, thinking. "Who do I know that's a criminal I can trust?" Then he laughed. "A criminal I can trust. That's a good one." He rifled through my things, went into the pockets of all my clothes, combed through the contacts on my phone. Then, he found it: the business card of my Filipino banker, Alejo Reyes at the Banco Nacional de Manila. I read his body language: *This is it!* He clasped the card to his chest and raised his face skyward, eyes closed, wordlessly thanking the patron saint of criminals.

Now, what to do with my body? He would never be able to smuggle it out of the hotel, he had no car, he had no money —only those damned bonds. He went outside onto the balcony which overlooked Wilshire Boulevard. As always, it was choked with traffic in both directions. Then it came to him. He went through my pockets and found a few dollars in cash. Then, he went out and bought some hair dye—brown for him and blond for me. After dying his hair brown, he spent a lot of time in the mirror with his makeup kit, getting that little bump in his nose just right. Then, he dragged me into the bathroom, laid me out in the bathtub, and dyed my hair blond—his shade. I saw what he was planning. He dressed my body in his clothes and planted all his IDs on it. I—or rather Rodney French—was going to commit a spectacular suicide on Wilshire Boulevard.

Timing was everything. He had to wait until morning—banking hours—to go see Alejo. The suicide had to take place just as he left the hotel. He knew my body would soon be identified, but this would provide a great diversion as he made his escape. There must be no evidence left behind. No trace of me; no trace of Rodney. He spent the rest of the night wiping the place clean of fingerprints, putting every object back exactly where it was. The sheets would bear forensic evidence, and the place would be crawling with cops after I "jumped," so he stripped the bed, took all the sheets, pillowcases and blankets, and threw them down a laundry chute at 2 a.m. He wouldn't bother to check out of the hotel. They already had my credit card on file. He would just get into one of the cabs that were always outside and take it to the bank.

*

Meanwhile, back in New York, Hereford Stanley had discovered the bonds—and me—missing. They called the SEC, the FBI, and their lawyers. The search was on. It didn't take the FBI long to track my credit card to the airline, to LA, to the hotel. They arrived just in time for Rodney's "suicide." Undeterred, they went up to our room, literally rubbing shoulders with Rodney as he left the hotel. He would have to use my credit card for the taxi. I went along for the ride. "What's all the commotion?" he asked the cab driver.

"Some guy jumped off a balcony and splattered all over the sidewalk. Good thing he didn't land on anybody."

At the Banco Nacional, Rodney introduced himself to Alejo as me. He didn't know whether or not Alejo and I had actually spoken before. We had — on the phone. Alejo detected something fishy, a different voice perhaps. He gave Rodney a funny look, then brightened and said, "Of course! Come this way." Rodney followed Alejo into his private office, where Rodney turned over the bonds. "Just one moment," said Alejo. And he left the room. He returned a few moments later with a large suitcase with wheels — full of cash. "Here you are, fourteen million less my commission of two million. Twelve million dollars. Have a nice trip." Rodney didn't blink. He took the money with a smile, briefly surveyed it to make sure the money was real (it would take days to count it). Now, Alejo knew he wasn't me. The commission was only supposed to be one million. Rodney took a hundred-dollar bill out of the suitcase, went to a bank teller and had her break it into smaller bills, then he left the bank to hail a cab, dragging the suitcase — which weighed nearly 300 pounds — behind him. He didn't know how hard it is to hail a cab in LA.

There were a lot of things Rodney didn't know. He sure was pretty, but not much between the ears. For instance, he didn't realize that $12 million in cash weighs 264 pounds. Of course, I had considered all of this in my plan. This is where my accomplice, Otto Gorshenheim, comes in. Otto was an old and trusted friend who owned a thriving antique shop in Beverly Hills. I knew I couldn't get a 300-pound suitcase loaded with cash onto a plane and across an international border. No one could. So, Otto — for a generous cut of the profits — was going to send me a series of antiques in Thailand: urns, statues, lamps, all stuffed with cash. Each would be carefully packed and impervious to x-ray detection. I would receive my money, one million at a time.

Rodney was in big trouble. The FBI had already traced

his use of my credit card in the taxi he took to the bank. They had the address and they were on their way. But it wasn't the feds who picked him up on the street outside the bank; it was a car full of Filipino gangsters. They whisked him into the back seat and knocked him unconscious. It took three strapping guys to lift the suitcase into the trunk. I got into the car with them. It was crowded, but I didn't take up much space. Then, they put a bullet through Rodney's feeble brain and threw his body out of the car in an alley.

As soon as Rodney's soul left his body, I began to feel an odd tingling. I was spinning inside a vortex of some kind. Rodney was with me; we were nose-to-nose. We spun for what seemed forever until we were abruptly plunked down, down, down into a dark place. As my eyes adjusted, I could see we were in a cramped prison cell. I had a sick, sinking feeling. *So, there is a hell after all.* It was just me and Rodney. Rodney and me. Glaring at each other. *Is this how I spend eternity?*

THE LITTLEST GHOST

My mother wasn't an evil person, just an idiot. She was so self-absorbed, so feeble-brained that she forgot to roll the window down when she left me in the car that hot summer day and went to have her hair done. I was only six months old, all trussed up in that car seat, and the heat in the car literally cooked me. Not a good way to die for a little baby.

When I had that little body, all I could do was gurgle, say goo-goo and ga-ga, but now that my soul was liberated, I was in touch with all the wisdom of my 546 lifetimes. My time in Egypt in 2074 B.C., my time with the Buddha in Lumbini and India, living through the Black Plague in Europe, assisting Michelangelo in the Sistine Chapel. That short life in Apache Junction, Arizona was a comparative waste of time. I'm glad it was so short.

Gliding though the ether, I wondered what was in store for me next. As if in answer to my musings, I came upon a mountain-sized pyramid. It was built in the style of the ancient Mayan pyramids, like a giant four-sided staircase, but made out of shiny black marble. On top was a glistening pool of water. The Oracle Pool. I remembered it from my past deaths. I alighted beside the pool, which was a round bowl scooped out of the flat, square marble. I looked into the mirror-still water and saw that my soul still wore the veneer of my baby boy body. My reflection spoke to me: "You must return to earth and visit your mother. She was arrested for accidentally killing you, but is now out on parole. She is thinking of having another baby. This woman has the brain of a sixteen-year-old and the emotional maturity of a twelve-year-old. She is not capable of being a mother. You must dissuade her. Scare her, haunt her, do whatever it takes, but *do not let her conceive."*

*

While my father was fighting in the Afghanistan War, my mother, Loretta, who was quite an attractive woman, had taken up with Lenny, a sociopathic drug dealer. Both he and my father were violent and abusive men, taking out their rage at their own deficiencies on my mother. They were as unfit to be fathers as Loretta was to be a mother.

Back in Apache Junction, my mom was happily hallucinating in her bedroom in Lenny's lush condo. Lenny had gotten her hooked on the synthetic opioids he peddled. It kept her out of his hair. The mercury on the thermometer outside read 110 degrees, but in Loretta's air-conditioned bedroom it was cool and dark. That's when I appeared, floating above her.

"*Oooooo, oooooo!*" I tried to make ghost sounds and made scary gestures with my pudgy hands.

"Tommy! Oh, Tommy. Where have you been? I've been looking all over for you."

I could see my ghost act was not scaring her. She was too stoned. I tried a different tack. I added a guilt-inducing echo effect to my voice:

"Mommy! Mommy! You killed me. Your own little baby boy. Remember?"

"I'm sorry, Tommy, I didn't mean it. It was an 'accidently.' I'm such a jellyhead."

She laughed an embarrassed laugh.

My father, Tom, for whom I was named, kept writing letters from Afghanistan. He also tried to call, but Loretta would never answer her phone. He wrote to the shabby apartment he and Loretta had occupied when he left. Loretta only kept the place to get the checks sent by the military and for a place to go when Lenny would throw her out. Tom kept asking for new photos of me and asking why she didn't return his calls. She never told him I was dead. That would surely make him very mad. Probably mad enough to come back and kill her. Now there was a thought. But I didn't suppose the Higher Powers would approve of me solving the problem by getting her murdered. And, of course, Tom would be arrested and, no doubt, executed.

I decided to go away and come back when Loretta wasn't high. But Lenny kept her high all the time. Otherwise, she would drive him crazy with her inane chatter and trying to get him to knock her up.

Lenny was a dark, brooding brute of a man. A loner. He busied himself bagging up his main product, a white powder called China White, into various sizes: $10 for a single dose, $20 for two. You'd get a discount at $50 — six for $50. China White was a concoction of a synthetic opioid called α-methylfentanyl combined with a little heroin. He got this drug from a defrocked pharmacist named Schuster who, in turn, got it from China via Mexico. Lenny bought it in bulk and, now that so many were in the throes of addiction, Lenny was making a killing—sometimes literally. His customers occasionally died of overdoses. But there were always more to fill their shoes.

Lenny never did China White or opioids. "Don't get high on your own supply." That was his not-very-original motto. His drug of choice was cocaine. He was always snorting from a small glass vial with a tiny spoon attached to the top.

One of Lenny's O.D. victims was a young man named Billy Joe Hardwell. After Billy Joe died, his girlfriend, Tina, a pretty girl of eighteen, vowed revenge on Lenny, but she didn't have a clue as to how to do it.

I petitioned the Higher Powers for a conference with Billy Joe. I knew if he whispered in Tina's ear, she would hear him. My petition was granted, and Billy Joe met me at the Oracle Pool atop the onyx pyramid. I suggested a plan to Billy Joe and he, in turn, suggested it to Tina.

She started coming around to Lenny's, flirting with him. As usual, Loretta was in her bedroom, so out of it she didn't even know Tina was there. Tina would come over and snort coke with Lenny. She never let him have sex with her, but he always tried, and she always dangled the possibility. "Maybe next time," she'd say. Then one night, she switched Lenny's vial of coke with an identical vial containing about a gram of China White, which was about 100 times stronger than heroin. It was the stuff that had killed Billy Joe. Lenny did a big "one-and-one," his brow furrowed. "This coke smells funny," he said. He did another couple of hits, then offered it to Tina. Tina smiled a little smile, shook her head, watched him swoon and lose consciousness. The drug causes respiratory depression, and Tina waited until she was sure Lenny was dead.

It wasn't until the next day that Loretta awoke from her stupor and discovered the body. She panicked, packed all her things, and went back to her old apartment—just in time to greet my father, who had returned unexpectedly, worried that he hadn't heard from her. Now Loretta had to tell Tom the truth about me, how she had accidentally killed me. As I had predicted, Tom, who always had a gun handy, shot my mother dead. I was there to greet her as she crossed over. I gave her a good talking-to—told her to quit being such a jellyhead. And, as I had predicted, Tom was arrested, tried, and executed, so he soon joined us.

Now the whole family is together again. I wonder why. I pray to the Powers: *Please don't make me go through another lifetime with these idiots.*

BETRAYAL

When I was alive on earth, I looked at my life as a series of betrayals. I looked at myself as a victim, a victim of circumstances and people.

When I was very young, my mother, who was a concert violinist, quashed my ambitions to be a musician by cruelly telling me I sang out of tune. Who does that to a four-year-old? My mother. I shifted my focus to painting and then writing. I desperately wanted my mother's approval. She liked it when I brought home degrees, so I brought her two masters degrees: one in fine art and one in creative writing. I taught both subjects in a couple of colleges and became editor in chief of an arts magazine at an Ivy League college.

My first husband, Roger, was a tall, ectomorphic brit with flaming red hair. I was eighteen when we were married. I was madly in love with him and for several years we were happy. Well, I was never completely happy. There was always some impediment to my complete happiness. I was plagued by a myriad of physical problems, some may have had emotional causes, although at the time I would never admit to that possibility. I was given to panic attacks. My throat would close up and I had phobias of elevators and airplanes. (Living in an apartment in New York City, elevators were hard to avoid.) I was also afflicted with fibromyalgia, vertigo, migraines, and hypertension. And then, of course, there was the constant depression. I blamed all of this on people and things around me, never on myself.

Then, five years into our marriage, Roger took to drink. His father was an alcoholic and I guess the disease caught up with him. One night, we went to a party at the home of Diana, a girl I had known since high school. Diana was always envious of me, of my brains, of my boobs. She always coveted my boyfriends for no other reason than that I had them and she didn't. I didn't want to go to her party but Roger did, so we went. Diana hadn't changed much; she was as acidic as ever. I got a headache and left early; Roger stayed, getting more and more plastered. I took a cab home and waited. I waited two hours, then went back. Some of the partiers were still there, snorting cocaine off the living room coffee table. I didn't know them, but they let me in. I walked into Diana's bedroom and found Roger in bed, naked, with Diana and another girl. I told him not to bother coming home. His wealthy father in England offered me $20,000 not to divorce him. That was big money in the 1970s. I refused.

Next, a few years later, came Eran, a handsome and clever Israeli. He was a successful importer of Persian rugs made in Afghanistan. He was gregarious, funny, and entertaining. But he was very strident and liked to argue. He gave me terrible headaches, so I suggested he take a trip. He went to Europe, met another woman, and divorced me.

All the while, I was trying to get pregnant. I wanted a baby more than anything. I had four miscarriages during my first two marriages. The doctors said my uterus was too "fibrous" to host a fetus. Then I met Lloyd, a photographer whose work I used in the magazine. He was the best lover I'd ever had and soon I was pregnant again. I was a few years older than he, in my mid-forties by then. But this baby hung in there. He was a tough little bulldog and continued that way long after he had exited my inhospitable womb.

I named him Fyodor, after Dostoyevsky, my favorite author. Lloyd objected strenuously, insisting a name like that would be a stigma for the child, would make other kids treat him like a foreigner, a freak. In retrospect, I have to admit he was right, but I was intractable.

Lloyd (and his mother) were very anxious for us to get married. I was reluctant. Deep down, I really didn't love Lloyd. But, for the sake of Fyodor and Lloyd's mother (my own mother had died a few months earlier—and I still had not recovered from that), I agreed.

At first, we were doing alright financially. I now had a job teaching at a small private college on Long Island. I had taken a big salary cut from my glory days, but I had made some smart investments and I had considerable savings. Lloyd had a photography studio. I knew he was struggling to stay afloat, but I didn't know how bad it was until later.

I was a gifted teacher, imparting to young, aspiring writers my passion for words and the English language. My classes were always full, and there was a waiting list to sign up. After three years of this, I was summarily fired. I knew it was just because my colleagues were envious of me, of my popularity with the students. The official reason, however, was that I had made a crack in class, telling some girl she wrote like the illegitimate offspring of Mickey Spillane and Jackie Collins. It was intended to be just a light-hearted jest. The class laughed; the girl did not. She complained to the head of the English department and, to coin a phrase, that's all she wrote (ha ha).

About this time, I found out that—unbeknownst to me —Lloyd had run up my credit card to the tune of $90,000 in an effort to save his foundering business. It drove me to bankruptcy. I was furious beyond words. I never saw any of the bills from the credit card company. Later, as I vented about this to a friend, she asked: "Didn't you wonder why you never saw a bill?"

"Lloyd always grabbed the mail before I saw it," was my reply.

He was also supposedly taking care of the storage unit where my parents' priceless antiques were stored. I didn't find out that he wasn't until all my family's historic possessions were sold at auction. I didn't speak to Lloyd for a year, except to ask him to move out.

He never did, and by this time, I was always so sick I couldn't work and rarely got out of bed. So Lloyd had to go to work in a camera store by day and work from home as a copy editor by night. He also made all my meals and served them to me in bed. I stayed married to him and lived with him for the rest of my life, but I never let him in my bed again. He slept on the couch for thirty-five years. He paid the rent and the bills (mostly). Once, when they turned off our electricity, I had to ask my old friend Eddie to send me the money. I spoke to a few old friends on the telephone and we exchanged emails. My best friends were Eddie in California and Linda in North Carolina, both of whom I had been in college with. I had known Eddie back in high school. They were both great admirers of my towering intellect and my many artistic talents. At first, they commiserated with me over my multiple misfortunes.

Meanwhile, Fyodor had grown up. He was mostly away at college—until Lloyd failed to pay the tuition and he got kicked out. I had to intervene and set up a payment plan. Finally, he was able to finish and graduate. When he came home, he insisted on being called Fred. He lived in our small apartment with us for a few years after his graduation, earning a little money as a sales clerk in a bookshop. "Fred" was furious at both of us, but mostly at me. For some reason, he held me responsible for all the discord in our family and all the terrible financial debacles that had befallen us. He didn't believe I was really sick and incapable of getting a job. He believed it was all psychosomatic. He shunned me for long periods. That crushed me, perhaps more than anything.

I became more and more reliant on my conversations with Eddie. We were both now in our sixties. He lived alone, having survived three marriages, and so we took mutual comfort in our conversations. We cracked jokes, sang Beatles songs, and he listened to my tales of woe. He admired my razor-sharp wit. Then, he met someone on an online dating site. She was fifty, beautiful, and wealthy, he said. They had fallen in love, he said. I heard from him less and less. He now had little time for our long, nocturnal repartee.

After a year, she dumped him. He was blindsided—never saw it coming. She said she loved him, but she needed someone with more money. As much as she had. Now he was calling me every night crying his eyes out. He was crushed. I was his only source of comfort. And I was there for him. If I harbored resentment for the year he had abandoned me, I didn't show it.

My bouts with the very real and excruciating pain of fibromyalgia and frequent fevers and migraines were making me ill-tempered and resentful. But whom did I resent? Everyone. The whole world for leaving me in this awful place. Soon, my constant complaints and woes were wearing thin on my good friends. Linda told me, a bit irritably, to either forgive Lloyd or leave him.

Eddie was now working as a copywriter at an advertising agency and was beginning to fancy himself an author. He was writing a short story, and he asked me to lend him my expertise in the world of haute couture, a subject he knew nothing about and I knew everything about. Eddie was a very talented songwriter and musician and I frequently praised his work in that arena. But, when he crossed over into literature—my arena —I was resentful. When he asked me for feedback and expertise, I was reticent to give it away for free. I was practically starving, and he had a pretty good job, why shouldn't he pay me for my expertise? He offered to send me $100; I was scornful. After one particularly ugly email exchange, Eddie called me up and told me he didn't want anything more to do with me. He said I had been using our very long-standing friendship as an excuse to be abusive and disrespectful. He excommunicated me from his life. At about the same time, Linda stopped responding to my emails and didn't answer my phone calls. I was heartbroken — and also angry. I sent out a barrage of vitriolic emails. I kept reminding Eddie of how I had been there for him after his girlfriend burst his bubble. He admitted to neglecting me when he was happy and then leaning on me when he was desolate, and he'd apologized for that, many times. But I just kept on throwing it in his face. I thought Eddie and Linda had conspired to abandon me. But from here I could see they hadn't.

The years went by. Fyodor got a better job and moved into his own apartment. I saw very little of him. Lloyd continued to work two jobs and do all the cooking and cleaning for me. I stayed in bed, except for the occasional doctor's appointment. I hardly had any friends left. I spoke on the phone to two people I had known a long time, but who were quite boring and annoying. They just wanted to talk about their problems.

I started seeing a psychiatrist, but he really didn't make me see myself any more clearly. After years of no contact, I emailed Eddie and Linda. I told them they should have done an intervention with me when I went off the rails. I told them I was now getting professional help and I was much better. Then I railed at them some more for breaking my heart. But no apology, no *mea culpa*. I told them I was dying, but no response from either of them. It turned out I *was* dying.

In my many conversations with Eddie, who was a self-styled Buddhist, he talked that old hippie talk about reincarnation and karma. I told him I believed only in what I could see, hear, and touch in this, the physical universe, and that, when you die, it's just nothing. Consciousness ceases. Kaput. Done.

It turns out I was wrong. I'm not sure if he was completely right, but he was closer than me. Now I sit in a misty netherworld and ceaselessly review my life. I can see it — not like myself — but objectively, like another person. I don't know what happens next, but I hope I get another bite at the apple.

SHOP TILL YOU DROP

I was at Bergdorf Goodman, in the lingerie department, looking at some positively divine camisoles, when there was a big commotion downstairs in the jewelry department. I peered down the escalator to see if I could tell what was going on. I saw a team of paramedics rush past. I decided to go down and find out what had happened, and who should I run into at the foot of the escalator, but Fanny Schlosser.

"Fanny! Fancy running into you here. What a cute outfit; where did you get it?"

"Right here."

"Do you know what happened?" By now our view was blocked by a crowd of people who had gathered. A policeman made them all step back to give the paramedics room to work. Fanny and I walked to the outside of the circle and peered in.

"I think some woman had a heart attack," said Fanny.

It was then I remembered. Fanny was dead. "Fanny, umm, didn't I attend your funeral last March?"

"Did you? How sweet of you, Elaine. You always were a good friend."

"But that means — you're dead."

"Uh-huh. And so are you. Take a look..."

We elbowed our way through the crowd. It was like cutting butter with a hot knife. They didn't even feel us. And there, being loaded onto a stretcher was ME. Well, my body at any rate. I caught a glimpse of my own lifeless face, just before they pulled the blanket over it.

"Oh my. This is really going to throw a wrench into Ben's golf weekend... So now what happens?" I assumed that, by now, Fanny had figured out how things work in the afterlife. "Do you go to heaven if you've been good and hell if you've been bad?"

"Well," said Fanny, "as far as I can tell, most people were neither all that good nor all that bad. Average people—like us—we go on with an existence that's not too different from when we were alive. Like, when you were alive, what was your favorite activity?"

"Shopping, of course."

"Of course. Me too. And so, here we are at Bergdorf Goodman. We can buy anything we want. And—get this—our credit cards never max out."

"Then there is a heaven," I exclaimed.

"Well..." said Fanny.

"What? What's the catch? I knew there was a catch."

"The catch is we never get to leave the store. We can buy all the most glamorous clothes and accessories we want. We can even wear them (she indicated the outfit she was wearing). But only here, in Bergdorf Goodman."

"Ugh. Where's the fun in that?"

"Exactly."

"And what do we do with all the stuff we accumulate? Where do we keep it?"

"Come on, I'll show you..."

She led me to a door marked PRIVATE. God knows I've been in Bergdorf Goodman enough to know every nook and cranny and I had never noticed this door before. As soon as her hand touched the knob, there was an unlocking sound and we entered what appeared to be the lobby of a luxury hotel.

"My goodness," I said, "I never dreamed this was here."

We approached the reception desk. Behind it stood a nondescript, middle-aged bald man with glasses.

"Hello, Charlie," said Fanny. "We need a room for Elaine here. Just arrived. Heart attack. Right here in the jewelry department. Can you believe it?"

"Welcome, Elaine," said Charlie. "How convenient for you. You didn't even need to go to the hospital. Lucky you. You can catch all kinds of horrible germs in hospitals."

"I know," I said.

Charlie handed me a key card with a number on it: 47. "I gave you one right near Fanny."

"Thanks, Charlie," said Fanny. Then to me: "I'm in fifty-one. Just my age when I died, ha ha."

"Hey, that's funny. I'm forty-seven now."

"And forever," said Fanny. "I see you already have quite a few packages—and so do I—so let's go up and put our things away now. I can show you my collection."

I noticed the lobby had quite a few shoppers coming and going; entering the three elevators laden with Bergdorf Goodman shopping bags and leaving empty-handed, heading back out the door through which we had entered, faces aglow with anticipation of the new acquisitions that awaited them.

"Are they all dead like us?" I asked Fanny.

"Oh, yes indeed."

"They certainly look happy."

"Yes, some people never get tired of it," said Fanny. And she let out a little sigh.

The elevator took us up to the second floor. We walked down a long corridor.

"Here's my place," said Fanny when we came to number fifty-one. "Come on in."

The room was vast. So much larger than the hotel room I was expecting. There were no windows. Along three walls were closets with sliding doors, all of which had floor-to-ceiling mirrors. The rest of the room, which was somewhere around 1,000 square feet, was almost filled with items for the home, all still in their boxes: vases, objets d'art, crystal glassware, some kind of cutting board, chocolate cigars…

"Wow," I said. And you've only been here since last March? You've certainly acquired a lot of stuff!"

"Yes," said Fanny. "It's pretty hard to resist having the stuff you've always wanted when it's all free. Now, hold onto your hat…" And she opened the sliding closet doors, revealing rack upon rack of gorgeous designer dresses, tops, skirts, coats, hats, all neatly arranged according to category, season, etc. There were built-in drawers for sweaters and pullovers. And the top drawers were for jewelry. Fanny opened one. It nearly knocked my eyes out. It was lined in black velvet and looked like a display case in a high-end jewelry store. I beheld row upon row of necklaces, rings, watches, broaches, pendants. Mostly diamonds and gold. Each item was neatly nestled in its own custom-molded black velvet niche. Then she closed it really fast.

"Whoa! Can I see that again?"

"Later," she said.

Then she opened the shoe closets. I was dazzled. Here were hundreds — maybe thousands — of fabulous shoes from all the greatest European designers. One pair attracted me instantly.

"Oh my God. Where did you get these?" They were the most elegant-yet-flashy pumps I had ever seen. They were an indescribable shade of blue and covered with sparkling facets that mimicked alligator scales.

"Why, here, of course. Where else?"

"Can I get some?"

"I'm afraid not, Elaine. You know how shoe lines go. Here today, next season discontinued. These are from last Spring. I was lucky. I got just about the last pair in my size. Then, pfft! Gone."

"Gone? You mean they're gone? I can't get them anymore? They're 'ungettable'?"

"Mm-hmm."

"What size do you wear?"

"Seven."

"Same as me! Can I ... try them on?"

"Forget it, Elaine. These are my very favorite shoes, and I'm not lending them to you or anyone."

"Oh please, Fanny. Just let me try them on. They match my eyes."

"No!"

"Fanny, I'll trade you anything for these shoes. Look at this..." I took off the diamond pendant from around my neck. "This was a gift from Ben on our first anniversary. Twenty-four karat gold with a four-karat diamond. It's worth—who knows—ten thousand? Maybe more..."

"Not a chance. I'm not parting with these shoes. Not while I—exist. No foot but mine will enter these shoes."

"I'm sorry, Fanny," I said, all the while wracking my brain as to how I could pry these shoes loose from Fanny's grasp, "Let's just forget about it. Is there anything else to do here besides shop and hoard? I don't see a bed. Do we sleep?"

"Never. We don't need sleep and we don't need food." She sighed again. "There's not much to look forward to here." Then she brightened. "But it's almost time for the Spring fashion show," she said excitedly.

"They hold fashion shows?"

"Yes. Twice a year. One for the Spring lines and one for the Fall lines. All the major fashion houses will be represented. And they have real models."

"Are they alive?"

"Of course not. These are strictly for the dead."

"You wouldn't think that many drop-dead-gorgeous young girls would—drop dead." I chuckled at my own joke.

"You'd be surprised," said Fanny. "Lots of models die of drug overdoses—mostly cocaine and amphetamines. Appetite suppressants. Of course, we don't have enough right here in

Bergdorf to provide enough models for a fashion show, so they fly them in. From Paris, I think. But they do like to include as many of the local residents as possible... Hey, you modeled when you were young, right?"

"Well ... not for very long." I didn't tell her that the very reason I quit was that I was developing a cocaine habit.

"You're still young and quite beautiful. You're a perfect size six, you're tall. Maybe you could try out to be a model."

Ordinarily, I wouldn't consider such a display of exhibitionism. But something about this idea made the wheels in my brain start to turn. "Okay. How do I do that?"

"We'll go see Monsieur Delacroix. He's the ladies clothing buyer for Bergdorf and the director of the fashion shows. A personal friend of mine. But first, let's take a look at your room."

We walked a few doors down the hall and I unlocked number forty-seven. It was exactly the same as Fanny's room, but dead empty. The emptiness of it made it look all the more enormous. On the far wall to the left was a sign. The same sign was bolted to the same wall in Fanny's room, but I hadn't bothered to read it: THE THREE COMMANDMENTS. The first two looked quite familiar: THOU SHALT NOT COVET THY NEIGHBOR'S GOODS, THOU SHALT NOT STEAL. The third one was different, and I wasn't sure what it meant: THOU SHALT SHOP UNTIL YOU STOP WANTING. I opened some of the mirrored closets. Completely empty. I dropped the few items I had purchased before my demise. "I'll put them away later. Let's get out of here. It's depressing."

"Meeting Monsieur Delacroix will cheer you up. He's a delightful man (gay, of course)," she whispered through the back of her hand as if there were someone there to overhear —or care.

Fanny took me to an office. One of several that were located on the mezzanine balcony that overlooked the lobby.

A tall, distinguished-looking Frenchman greeted us, impeccably dressed in an Armani suit and Hermès tie.

"*Allo, Fanny! Comment ça va?*" They air-kissed each other on both cheeks.

"*Oh, trés bien, trés, trés bien, Monsieur Delacroix — pour une personne mort.*" Monsieur Delacroix laughed uproariously. I didn't get it. Fanny had become quite the woman of the world since her death. "Monsieur Delacroix, this is my friend, Elaine Brixton."

He shook my hand. "*Enchanté, Elaine.*"

"*Enchanté,*" I repeated, exhausting most of my French with a single word.

"Elaine's a new arrival. She did some modeling in her youth. Do you think you could use her in the Spring fashion show?"

M. Delacroix stepped back with his hand on his chin and scrutinized me. "*Peut-être... peut-être...*" He took some pictures of me with his iPhone, then clapped his hands twice fast. Two women rushed out of nowhere. One had a tape measure and started taking my measurements. The other wrote them down on a little pad. M. Delacroix looked at the numbers, nodded, and said he would let me know. I thanked him and we left.

Then we shopped. And shopped. And shopped. My storage space was beginning to fill up. I would put on my new outfits and jewelry and parade, as if on a runway, up and back, watching myself in the long row of mirrors that were my closet doors. It was great not to have to worry about getting fat.

A few days later Charlie handed me a note from M. Delacroix:

> *Ma cher* Elaine, we will be pleased to have you try out as one of our resident models in the Spring fashion show, to be held ...

He put a date and time, but I had lost all track of time. He told me to show up in the Grand Ballroom for the "tryouts and try-ons" in three days.

I had never noticed before, but there were three corridors leading off the main lobby of our "hotel." Each had signs, indicating different rooms, like in a hotel. There was the Intelligent Design Room, the Eternity Room, and then there was the Grand Ballroom, the largest of all, where the fashion show would be held.

Now I really started practicing in earnest. Fanny would come over and coach me. I was starting to look pretty good. It felt great to have a project besides shopping. I was glad Fanny had goaded me into volunteering against my better judgment. And, all the while, a plan was beginning to hatch in my brain...

From time to time I would go to the ground floor of Bergdorf Goodman and wander over to the entrance door. I would look out the display windows — the only windows in the store — and view the passing parade of the living outside on Fifth Avenue. Then I would casually try the door. I could neither push nor pull it, although a constant stream of living shoppers passed through it with ease in both directions. My hands couldn't even grasp the brass handles. They just passed through them, as if they were made of air. Or I was.

I noticed that one of the three elevators had a "B" button below the "L" for the lobby. Basement? I wondered what was down there, and if it could be a possible escape route. I pressed it, the doors closed and I went down one floor. The doors opened. I stepped out into what looked like a department store basement. There was a room marked BOILER ROOM. I opened the door and looked inside to see giant boilers being stoked with coal by skeletal laborers. No, this was not a promising route. The basement itself was a long corridor. More skeletons labored here. An aluminum laundry chute loaded large canvas laundry carts with piles of clothing: last year's returns, old and soiled clothes... They formed two lanes: one headed for an open doorway with full carts, the other returning with empty carts. I followed one of the full carts to a ramp that led up to a loading dock in an alley. The skeleton worker, heedless of me, pushed his cart up the ramp, to the edge of the loading dock, and tipped it over. All the clothing fell into the back of a giant dump truck. I walked out onto the loading dock—into fresh air. I was free. None of the skeletons seemed to notice me. This was my escape route. I could walk away from Bergdorf Goodman this minute if I wanted to. But I wasn't quite ready just yet...

※

At last, the day of the tryouts arrived. The resident models —those who were not flown in from somewhere but resided here at Bergdorf—assembled in the Grand Ballroom and were taken backstage. There were racks of designer dresses, tops, skirts, blouses and coats, all new arrivals for Spring. Each rack had the sizes clearly marked with a sign at either end.

Fanny was allowed to accompany me, as my "fashion advisor." I immediately went to the size six dresses. There were at least fifty dresses to choose from. Unlike the professional models, we would be allowed to choose the item we modeled. We were each allowed only one item. I quickly leafed through the dresses and then stopped. There it was: just what I was looking for. It was a blue sheath by Roberto Cavalli, made out of a wonderful sparkly fabric. It matched my eyes. I quickly stripped off the dress I was wearing and tried it on. It fit like it was made for me. No alterations could have improved the way I looked in that dress. I turned to Fanny. She was clearly impressed.

"This is it," I said.

All she could say was "Mm-hmm."

"Fanny, I'm going to ask you a question. Don't answer

right away. I want you to think about it. This dress matches those shoes of yours like they were made for each other. You can see that, can't you?"

"Mmm hmm."

"Please, please, please, can I borrow them. Just for the show?"

Fanny was silent for what seemed like an eternity. "Okay," she said at last.

I hugged her with all my might. "Oh thank you, Fanny darling. You are truly my best friend, living or dead."

"Please, you're crushing my bustier," she said.

I approached M. Delacroix. "Is it okay if I model this one, Monsieur Delacroix? Fanny's going to lend me shoes that match perfectly."

M. Delacroix stood back, appraising me in the dress. At last, he said "Beautiful."

"Oh thank you, thank you. I can't wait. I've been practicing."

"Well, keep practicing," he said.

Fanny and I jumped around like a couple of schoolgirls who'd just made the cheerleading squad.

Finally, the day of the show rolled around. The pros went on first, striding down the runway like they owned it. They wore the latest fashions from all the top designers—at least the ones available at Bergdorf Goodman. The girls were gorgeous. They looked so lifelike; it was hard to believe they were dead like us. The runway was lined with spectators. Every dead shopper at Bergdorf was there, filling the Grand Ballroom to beyond capacity. M. Delacroix now announced the resident models would be next.

I was backstage with Fanny. My heart seemed to be pumping a mile a minute although, of course, that was impossible. My turn was coming up and I told Fanny to go out front, so she could tell me how I did. Fanny left and then it was my turn. I raised my chin up and strode the length of the runway with all the poise and elegance of a pro. I did a graceful turn at the far end, showing off the outfit from all sides, then strode back to considerable applause.

As soon as I arrived backstage, I set my plan in motion. People clustered about me, patting me on the back, shaking my hand. I just smiled and kept walking. Calmly and quietly, I exited the backstage area, then the ballroom, through a back door. I made my way through the corridors to the elevators and waited for the one with the "B" button. I got on and pressed "B." Just as before, the robot-like skeletons were at their drudgery, marching in lockstep, as if to a relentless drumbeat, slowly pushing their huge canvas carts filled with unwanted clothing. They took no notice of me. I joined their solemn procession, walking toward the loading dock. As I reached the door that led to the outside, suddenly a dark shape filled the doorway. It was M. Delacroix.

"Elaine, you have broken all three commandments. Do you know what this means?" I couldn't speak, so I just shook my head. "It means you are now doomed to spend eternity as one of these creatures, ceaselessly laboring, forever."

I tried to protest, to speak in my own defense, but I was voiceless. I looked at my hands. They were just bones. M. Delacroix held a small mirror up to my face. It was an eyeless skull. I tried to scream, but nothing came out.

※

Now I could hear the drum, a low, slow beat to which we all had to march. Although I was unable to make a sound or stop marching back and forth, my mind was still intact. I remembered everything that had happened, and I wept inside for breaking the heart of my only friend. The clothing kept on coming. It slid down through the chute and filled the carts. Mostly I paid no attention to the contents but, one day, I recognized the items that filled my cart. It was all Fanny's stuff. And the glittering blue shoes I had stolen were right on top. Of course, I had no use—nor any desire—for anything anymore, but I wondered what had become of Fanny.

As if he had read my mind, M. Delacroix appeared before me in the doorway once more. "If you are wondering about your friend, Fanny, don't. She's moved on to a much better place. She is without a body, and she is completely free. You see, she finally understood the Third Commandment: She stopped wanting."

POSSESSED AND REPOSSESSED

Donnie was always such a good boy. He was a star student all through elementary and high school. He got into Princeton, then UC Berkeley as a graduate student in psychology. He received his Master's Degree and was on his way to a doctorate when something went wrong. It was 1969. Berkeley was alive with rebellion—mostly against the Vietnam War but, you know, full of nonconformity and creativity. They didn't care about money, didn't plan for the future, nothing.

Donnie always had a creative streak running through him, and all this hippie stuff brought it out. Halfway through his doctoral program, he dropped out. He moved into a seedy hotel in Berkeley, the Berkeley Inn. It was right in the middle of the hippie zone. He met a guitar player and they started writing songs together. Donnie wrote the words; the other guy wrote the music. I never heard any of them, but I warned him: "You're gonna end up poor," I said.

"Maybe so, mom, but I gotta try." That's what he told me.

In a way, it was my fault. Many years ago, when Donnie was just a little boy, we used to go to a bungalow colony in the Catskills in the summer. We would put on musical shows —and I would write the songs. Well, actually I just put new words—funny words—to popular show tunes. The place was owned by a man named Oscar Blavitz, but everybody called him "Uncle O." So I wrote a song to the tune of "Bali Ha'i" from *South Pacific* called "Uncle O's Bungalows."

Here's how it went:

> *Uncle O's will call you*
> *When New York starts to schvitz*
> *We'll be here till the fall, too*
> *Uncle O's bungalows*

Oh, I wrote lots of 'em. So I guess Donnie got it from me.

Donnie's father, Al, was a big baby. He always tried to puff himself up to be more than he really was. He was a salesman, and when Donnie was little, he was away from home a lot. Later, he got a job in New York, selling women's clothing to department stores. He was always getting himself elected as president of things. He was president of the Rotary Club of South Brooklyn. He was president of the Millenary Wholesalers Association of New York. Both his parents were killed in a car crash when he was five, and he never got any older emotionally since that day.

He made lots of money, but he always gambled half of it away, which is why we could never buy a house. I always wanted a home of my own, but we had to stay in our small, rent-controlled apartment in Brooklyn. Al always talked loud, as if he knew everything, but, really, he knew very little. When Donnie was little, he thought his dad was a big hero. Al showed him a lot of medals he said he'd won in World War II. But in reality, he had bought them in army surplus stores. But, by the time Donnie was in high school, he had Al's number: just a short, fat, bald blowhard.

When Al heard Donnie had dropped out of school, he went nuts. He telephoned him in Berkeley and called him a bum, a failure. He told him, "Don't bother to come home until you straighten yourself out." So Donnie never came home again. He moved to Los Angeles. Now, he was trying to write screenplays for the movies. He wrote quite a few, came close once or twice, but he never succeeded in selling anything. He also wrote children's books in verse. He sent me one; I thought it was charming. But he never sold any of those either. I wanted to go to California and visit him, but Al refused to take me. And that's when I had the heart attack and died.

*

I guess everybody makes their own heaven or hell. I awoke in my old neighborhood in Brooklyn, in my parents' little grocery store. My mother and father were there, big as life, and my little brother, who died way too young. They had all died the same year, and I was heartbroken for years afterward. I was very close with my family, and now we were all reunited. And we were all young. I was just a girl, and I helped out in the store, just like I used to. This certainly was my idea of heaven.

Al lived on, well into his eighties. He moved to Florida and married a nice old lady who had lots of money. He got himself elected president of the Owners' Association of their condo down there. He spoke to Donnie once or twice but was always very mean to him when he found out he still wasn't making any money. Donnie told him he had gotten his MFCC certification, which meant he could take private clients for counseling. He made a little money that way, and he got a job as a substitute teacher in the LA Unified School District. Those things enabled him to pay the rent, but he never gave up on his dreams of being a paid writer. Al still called him a bum.

When Al was on his deathbed, he spoke with Donnie one last time. He was in pain and he was very bitter and angry. Al told Donnie, "You have a strong, young body, and it's going to waste. I could do great things with a body like that." And, with that, Al jumped out of his old, sick body and into Donnie's. "Now, that's more like it," said Al from Donnie's mouth. "I feel thirty years younger. Hell, I *am* thirty years younger!"

Donnie's girlfriend, Teresa, was there. She was psychic, and from the way Donnie was ranting in Al's voice, she knew that Donnie had been possessed. "Get out of there, old man!" she yelled.

"The hell I will," said Al.

That's when my mother told me what was going on in Donnie's body. "You've got to get down there and save your son," she told me. The next thing I knew, I was descending back to earth, to California, into Donnie's apartment. I saw him sitting there on the bed with Teresa, bragging the way Al always did. "Hey, little lady," he said to Teresa, "you're not half bad. I'm gonna show you what a *real* man is like."

As he reached for Teresa, I went in and grabbed Al's spirit. I yanked him, kicking and screaming, out of Donnie. Donnie returned to himself. He looked up and saw me. His jaw dropped in amazement. Teresa saw me too. I smiled down at them, holding Al in my arms like he was a baby. As we slowly ascended, Al got younger and younger, until he was that five-year-old who had lost his parents all those years ago.

HELL HATH NO FURY

The first thing I noticed was the pain was gone. When prostate cancer metastasizes to your bones, it hurts like hell.

A woman in a gray uniform was leading me up a flight of marble steps that led to a grand building—a temple, a museum, or perhaps a courthouse. As we climbed, I looked around at a utopian city of gleaming spires and spotless, tree-lined streets. People and strange beings walked here and there, but somehow none of it looked real. The architecture was a blend of Greco-Roman and Arthur C. Clarke.

The lobby of the building had a vaulted ceiling that soared 100 feet above us and was adorned with frescoes that rivaled the Sistine Chapel.

"That looks like it could have been done by Michelangelo," I remarked, indicating the ceiling.

"It was," the woman replied without turning around.

She led me up another long flight of stairs that hugged the curved marble wall, then down a seemingly endless corridor. She opened a pair of double oak doors that revealed what was obviously a courtroom. It was a modernistic version of the classic oak-paneled courts of Victorian England. Before me was the high wooden edifice of the judge's bench, long enough to accommodate at least five magistrates. To the right of the bench was the witness stand. There was a rail in front of the spectators' seating. In front of the rail was a long table with about fifteen chairs behind it. Then, against the right wall, there was the prisoner's dock, a raised wooden fortress about five feet square, with a bench inside. It was like a cage with ornate wooden bars on three sides, so the prisoner could see the entire courtroom but remain confined.

"You sit in there," said the officer, indicating the prisoner's dock. She was a dour woman in her thirties with cold blue eyes and no upper lip. "The arbitrators will be here presently." Then she was gone and I was alone in this vast room.

I did as I was told, climbed the few steps and sat in the wooden box. Now, for the first time, it began to dawn on me. I must be dead. But where was I? Heaven? Hell? Something in between?

I had to wait a long time, and, while I waited, I reflected on my life. That last year, my seventieth, was hell. With the cancer. Lying there in the hospital, alone, except for the doctors and nurses. No one visited me. None of the big shots from the studio, none of my movie star friends, no one. I wished then that I'd had children by at least one of my six wives. Of course, none of them came to visit me either.

But, when I was young, everything was great. I was a successful film director, living high on the hog in Hollywood. The studio brass and all the actors kissed my ass. I had power. I was rich and handsome. I could get any woman I wanted, and I wanted them all. I wondered who would occupy all those chairs.

The Hollywood community held a big memorial fête for me. That, they showed up for. They got to get up and make speeches about what a great guy I was. They got their script writers to write them. They recounted heartwarming and amusing stories about what a tough cookie I was, what a perfectionist in my work. But with a heart of gold, of course. None of them meant a word they said, but it was, after all, a great photo op.

*

I waited for what seemed like an eternity. My sense of time had changed, now that I was dead, so it was hard to say how long. At last, a creature that looked like a human-sized cockroach entered from a side door and took its place at a small desk just below and to the left of the judge's bench. On the desk was some kind of recording device with a keyboard.

"All rise," it said in perfect American English. Its mouth or face didn't move. I just heard the words in my head. "All" was just me, so I rose.

Three robed magistrates entered from the left side and took their places on the raised bench. One of them—the one on the right—was clearly a human woman in her sixties. The other two were creatures. The one in the middle had a reptilian appearance: a scaly hide and expressionless black orbs for eyes. The one on the left was of diminutive stature, had an outsized, hairless head, and enormous eyes—like the way aliens were often depicted in science fiction movies and accounts of alien abductions.

"What's this all about?" I asked.

"Shh! No talking until everyone arrives," said the creature in the center. Her voice was that of an old woman and, like the bailiff, did not move any part of her face when she spoke. This was apparently the Chief Arbitrator. The bailiff rose, approached the bench, and whispered something to her. She addressed the room:

"I'm told that three of the plaintiffs are already here." Then to the bailiff, sotto voce: "Bring them in."

The bailiff scuttled up the center aisle, exited through the main doors through which I had entered, and returned a moment later, followed by an old lady with long gray hair and blue eyes. She looked vaguely familiar. She must have been my age, or maybe even older. The bailiff led her to the witness stand. After scrutinizing her for a while, I realized this was my first wife, Helen.

"Helen?" I said. She turned to me. Her eyes were filled with tears and fury.

"Shh!" said all three of the arbitrators.

The bailiff exited again and returned with Jenna, my first love, and Eleanor, my second wife. They were both quite a bit younger. In fact, they looked pretty good, except for the needle marks on Jenna's arms and the gaping wounds on Eleanor's wrists.

"Jenna! Eleanor! What—"

"Shh!"

They took their seats opposite Helen and the arbitrators behind the long desk at the front of the courtroom. Now I faced all three of them—silent, hateful. The three arbitrators opened briefcases and busied themselves with some files. The only sound was the annoying sound of alien claws shuffling papers.

*

With my distorted sense of time, it is impossible to say how long I sat. Probably years. But, after a very long time, and many attempts to ask why I am here, only to be repeatedly shushed, the chairs were all filled. All six of my wives were there: Helen, Eleanor, Sherri, Susanne, Lotus, and Linda. And the two biggest loves of my life: Jenna and Robin. These were not wives, but girlfriends and, naturally, my love for them was more intense than it had been for any of my wives.

"Okay," said the Chief Arbitrator, "you first, Helen."

I threw a hissy fit. "No, no, no! *you* first, Madame Arbitrator! You need to tell me what we're all doing here. Why did we have to wait so long?"

"Very well, Mr. Ward," she said mildly. "This is a Truth and Reconciliation session. Everyone is compelled to tell the truth, the whole truth, and nothing but the truth here. There is no need to swear on a Bible. You have no choice. We had to wait to get started until everyone was dead. All these women have many grievances against you, Mr. Ward. And, if they are not resolved here and now, none of you will be able to move on to a higher plane of existence." She turned to Helen. "Helen…"

"Please, Madame Arbitrator," I said, "one more question?"

"Very well."

"I've figured out that we are dead. We are in the afterlife; is that right?"

"Yes."

"But—how shall I put this—some of the beings in this room, yourself included, ma'am, are clearly not human. How can this be?"

A hush fell over the courtroom. It was clear I was not the only human wondering about this.

"You Earthlings are so arrogant," said the Chief Arbitrator. "In a universe with trillions of galaxies and trillions upon trillions of stars, can you possibly have the temerity to believe that your puny planet is the only one that hosts sentient life?"

"But…"

"Did you think the afterlife would be segregated by planet of origin? Sorry, but here you will be expected to intermingle and relate with beings from all over the universe. The Universal Mind that created everything does not distinguish between species. We are all the same to the All-Seeing Eye. Everything that lives dies. And, when we die, we all wind up in the same place. Here. Does that answer your question?"

I simply nodded and hung my head.

"Helen…"

The bailiff led Helen to the witness stand. She looked old; very old. And tired. She sighed, looking at me with a mixture of hatred and despair.

"I lifted you up out of the gutter, Larry. Remember? You were a starving wannabee actor without a plot to piss on." She gave a quick, ironic snort of laughter at her own accidental pun. "I was a successful screenwriter. I had two hit movies under my belt. I was a player in Hollywood. I took you around; I introduced you to the right people. I got you your first job as an AD, which led to your stellar directing career. Remember, Larry?" I nodded sheepishly. I knew what was coming. "And then, once the bloom was off the rose, once you were a rising star, and I was an aging matron, you *dumped* me, Larry. Like a used Kleenex. For *her*." She indicated Jenna. "And, when I lay dying in the hospital, my body riddled with cancer, did you even come to see me? Did you even send an email?"

I couldn't look her in the eye. "We were ... estranged," I mumbled.

"I left you phone messages, I sent you emails. I just wanted to say goodbye and no hard feelings. But from you, *nothing*."

I hung my head. It was all true, what she said. I had been a bad person. A very selfish person.

Then the second female arbitrator, the Earth woman, spoke up: "Is that all, Helen?"

Helen looked nonplussed. "Well, I—"

"Yes?"

"I tried to have you killed."

I looked back at her, aghast.

"You and Jenna both. Somebody told me about a hit man who was having a two-for-one special. I gave him $5,000. But, obviously, he never did it. He ran off with my money. What an idiot. I should've paid half up front and half upon completion. I never was much of a businesswoman."

"Anything else?"

"Remember when I went to Europe to work on that film —what was it called—*Murder Italian Style*?"

I nodded. She was gone for almost three months.

"I had an affair—with an Italian cinematographer."

"Is that it?"

Helen hesitated and thought for a moment. "Yes."

"So," said the second arbitrator, "no one here is blameless, as we shall see. Jenna, you're next, I believe."

The bailiff, who walked upright on its hind legs, but had four other insectile appendages protruding from both sides of its body, escorted Helen to a seat and led Jenna to the witness stand.

"We had quite a ride, didn't we, Larry? It was the '80s. We were awash in coke and Quaaludes. I guess you thought it was your personal magnetism that attracted a girl like me. Ha! It was the drugs, Larry. And you pumped 'em into me like I was a '57 Buick. I had an addictive personality—but you knew that. Your ego told you I was addicted to you. My body told me I was addicted to the drugs. When I finally OD'd —remember?—you came home and found me unconscious. You thought I was dead. Well, you certainly didn't want the body of a dead girl in your luxurious Beverly Hills mansion, so you dumped it in an alley in Panorama City. But I wasn't dead. Not then. Somebody found me and called the paramedics. And I survived. But, for some reason, I just couldn't get you on the phone after that. When I came to your place, you had security guards turn me away. I could've made trouble for you—in the newspapers, with the police—but I wasn't brought up to be a snitch, so I let it go. I died of a heroin overdose in a third-rate hotel room on Hollywood Boulevard. You always knew how to reach me, but you never did. You were on to your next thrill ride—*her*." She indicated Eleanor.

"But Larry wasn't the first person to introduce you to drugs, was he, Jenna?" said the human lady arbitrator, glancing down at the papers she had before her.

"Well ... no," said Jenna. "I had been addicted to one

thing or another since high school. In fact, I got busted for drugs in high school and kicked out of school. Luckily, my looks held up, and I was able to get modeling jobs."

"That's all Jenna, you may step down." said the arbitrator. "Eleanor?"

Eleanor was a beautiful and talented actress. We met when she landed her first role in a major film, one of mine. It was a bit part, but she was luminous on screen. We began dating, and we really clicked—physically as well as emotionally. We moved in together, and, soon after, got married. She started helping me choose projects. She had a rare gift for taking a mediocre script and turning it into a masterpiece. I decided she needed to quit acting and just do this for me. I put the word out around town that anyone who gave her a part would be on my shit list. It worked like a charm. She was rejected at every audition. She never knew it was because of me. She just assumed she had no talent. She continued to break down scripts for me for the next few years but became increasingly despondent. One night, we went to see a pre-debut screening of *The Grifters*. Eleanor had played Myra (the role played by Annette Benning in the movie) in an early stage adaptation of the Jim Thompson novel a few years earlier. She had auditioned for the role in the film, and would have gotten it—if not for me. When she saw the movie, something in her snapped. She didn't say a word to me all the way home in the car.

She took to drinking. She would start early in the morning and stay drunk the whole day until she passed out. She was no good to me after that, so I filed for divorce. I always had prenups with my wives, so she was left with no income. A few months later, she was found dead in the bathroom of a cheap motel near the airport. She had slashed her wrists and bled to death in the bathtub. Now she stepped onto the witness stand.

"I want to call a witness," she said.

"That is your right," said the Chief Arbitrator. "Who is it?"

"Him."

She was pointing at me.

"Go ahead, Larry," she said, "we both know what you did. But I want to hear you tell it."

So I told it. The whole filthy tale. It made me feel ashamed, but also somehow cleaner. Maybe there was something to this "truth" thing...

I had never thought of myself as a bad person. I thought of myself as a pragmatist. I did some distasteful things, sure. Things I didn't enjoy doing. But, I told myself, it was all in the service of the work, the art.

Now the third arbitrator spoke—the "ET" guy. I knew he was a guy because he spoke in a male voice: "Is that all true, Eleanor? Just the way it happened, with nothing left out?"

There was a silence, so long and heavy you could cut it with a knife. At last, Eleanor spoke.

"No... Larry was never as big a shot as he thought he was. There are no secrets in Hollywood. Everybody knew he put the whammy on me, lots of people told me about it, and some even knuckled under to it. But *The Grifters* was produced by Martin Scorsese and directed by Stephen Frears, and they were not intimidated by Larry. They let me know straight out when they passed on me: it wasn't because of Larry's curse; it was just that Annette was a little better for the role than I was—but not by much. I lost it fair and square."

"Is that the whole truth, Eleanor? Nothing left out?"

"Not quite... I always knew Larry was holding my acting career back. I enjoyed the work I was doing with him. I was good with writing. But I was good at acting too. I could have hated him for pulling a sneaky move like that. But I couldn't..." Tears ran down her face. "You see, I knew he was bad ... but I loved him. All he had to do was ask, and I would have given up acting for him. I would have done anything." She broke down, crying, heartbroken, and was led off the stand.

An alarmed buzz erupted among the women at the long table.

"Silence!" cried the Chief Arbitrator.

I was shaken to the core. All this was news to me. All these years, thinking I was pulling the wool over her eyes, and all the time she knew all and said nothing. That was real love. Love I never deserved. I couldn't keep from crying. If only I knew then what I know now...

When it was Robin's turn, I testified that I had given her a venereal disease and didn't tell her I had it. It went unchecked for weeks and when it was finally discovered, the infection was so bad she had to have her ovaries removed.

This, too, turned out to be untrue. Robin testified that someone else had given her the disease, and she had given it to me. Another shock. A wave of mixed emotions came over me. There had been someone else — with a disease?

Of course, I had cheated on all of them. I cheated on Sherri with Suzanne. I cheated on Suzanne with Lotus, I cheated on Lotus with Linda. But they all cheated on me with other guys. Guys I knew nothing about.

*

After the final testimony, the arbitrators left the room to deliberate. We all waited in silence for another eternity. At length, Robin got up and walked over to the prisoner's dock. She looked up at me with tears in her eyes and whispered.

"I just want you to know I never stopped loving you —you bastard!"

My heart ached. I looked back at her with real love and compassion for the first time in my, er, life.

Now the arbitrators returned and took their places. The Chief Arbitrator spoke.

"Here is our decision. It is final and non-negotiable: You are all guilty of misconduct and unethical activities throughout your lives. Larry more than the women.

"All the women will live together in a large but ordinary house for a period of 800 years. You will take turns being the housekeeper, cook, and chauffeur for a week. During that week, you will occupy the servant's quarters and wait on all the others. You will maintain civil and even cordial relations with each other. If any conflicts arise, you must appear before us again and risk extending your sentence. You must all remain celibate, and spend your days in quiet contemplation. Once a week, a different spiritual teacher will come and share his or her wisdom with all of you on how to evolve spiritually.

"Larry, you are sentenced to live 800 years in an austere monastery, where you will have a stone cell, a hard bed, and nothing but the bare necessities of existence. During the days, you will work as a gardener, a janitor, any menial job your superiors assign to you. You too will receive spiritual instruction."

Then she addressed everyone: "When your sentences are up, if you have conducted yourselves in a humble, respectful manner, done everything that was asked of you, and never complained, you will be permitted to move on to a higher plane of existence, where you will shed your bodies and merge with the Infinite. That is all."

The arbitrators rose as one, turned, and left the room.

*

I won't say it was an easy 800 years. There were many harsh lessons to be learned. The big one for me was humility, and I have learned it well.

FOR ALL ETERNITY

When Sarah died, we had been married for fifty years. At twenty-three, she was a dazzling beauty. Many men were vying for her attention. There was one, in particular, Roland, a tall, dashing Frenchman, and I knew she was attracted to him. He was rich, handsome, and erudite. He proposed to her. He wanted them to live together in Paris, but she had strong family ties in New York, and so I won the contest. When she agreed to marry me, it was the happiest day of my life. And every day after that was just as happy. Even after the heat and passion of youth cooled, she was everything to me, my center. Then the stroke hit. It left her completely paralyzed. She always made me promise not to let her die in a hospital, and so I ministered to her as best I could for that last week. Finally, mercifully, she slipped away. Before they came to take her lifeless body from our bed, I made the decision.

"I'm coming with you, my darling," I whispered.

Then I lay down beside her and took a dozen of her strongest pain pills. It was a very pleasant way to go. I highly recommend it.

*

When I awoke, I was standing on a dock, squeezed in on all sides by strangers. The crowd was enormous. Moored at the dock was a big white cruise ship. It looked like a giant, ship-shaped layer cake. People were boarding, going up a long gangplank, one by one. I couldn't see what was making the process so slow, but it was clear everyone wanted to get on board that ship. I doubted there would be room for everyone on the dock. I scanned the crowd, frantically searching for Sarah. I saw someone who looked like her from the back.

"Sarah, Sarah!" I cried. But it was not her.

I couldn't be too far behind her; she had only been dead an hour when I followed. Looking around, I noticed that no one in the crowd looked old. Everyone seemed to be in the prime of life. I looked at my hands, and they were young. Eventually, I got close enough to see that people in uniforms were making everyone form a line. We entered a terminal, walking single file between two ropes.

Inside, each aspiring passenger had to pass through a scanner, like the ones they use at airports to detect bombs or guns. But this scanner was scanning for something else. I believe it was scanning for character. As each person passed through, he or she was either allowed to ascend the gangplank or moved aside. The crowd of those who had been rejected was very large, and they looked unhappy and worried. I wondered what would happen to them. I wondered with dread if I would be one of them. I was sure Sarah was on that ship, and I didn't want her to sail without me. Then, in that sea of distraught faces—those who had been moved aside—I saw her. It was the young, beautiful Sarah, the one I had married fifty years ago. I ducked under the rope and ran toward the crowd of rejects.

"Sarah!" She saw me and fought her way through the mob to the rope that held them in.

"Sam! How…"

"Sarah, why are you here? Why didn't they let you on the ship?"

"Because…" And she broke down crying. "Because I was unfaithful to you, my darling." She dissolved in tears.

I couldn't believe my ears. "No. That's impossible. We were so happy. All those years…" Then I saw Roland making his way through the crowd of rejects. He stood beside her.

"I'm sorry, Sam," he said to me. "Sorry you had to find out this way."

"How long… how long did it go on?" I stammered, barely able to form the words.

"Five years," said Sarah. "The first five years of our marriage."

Then, a uniformed guard gently guided me back to my place in the line. I was crying. It was my turn to enter the scanner. Inside, it was not like the ones at the airport. I found myself staring into a mirror, at the young me, the me of fifty years ago. My reflection was cheerful, not crying.

"Your character has been as close to blameless as anyone I've seen," It said to me. "Except for the suicide. Suicide is a big sin… However, since your motivation was not borne of cowardice, but of love, this sin will be forgiven. You may board."

"But I don't want to board," I said through my tears. "I want to go where Sarah goes."

"That's not possible," said my image in the mirror. "You must board."

And so it was that I became the first person in anyone's memory to board the ship to paradise with a heavy heart. As I went up the gangplank, I looked back at the crowd of rejects. Sarah and Roland were at the front, and they waved a sad goodbye.

When I said I would love her for all eternity I didn't lie.

GHOST ACADEMY

I woke up on a park bench. I wasn't especially surprised, as that's where I had fallen asleep. But then I looked around. I wasn't in Detroit anymore. It wasn't cold anymore. I was in a vast and beautiful city, filled with crystal spires and marble minarets. My bench was in a lovely park, dotted with large stone sculptures, some recognizable, some strange and alien. Across the street was a great building with a wide, stone staircase leading to a portico. There were Greco-Roman columns, but there were modern and art deco elements as well. On the sidewalk, people, animals, and weird otherworldly creatures sauntered by at a leisurely pace, taking no notice of me. In the street beyond there were no cars, but wraith-like ephemeral beings flew by in both directions at great speeds. Above the massive Ionic columns, some words were inscribed in the triangular edifice: HALL OF KNOWING.

※

My name is Richard Partridge. I am the only son of a Black auto worker. (I refer to myself as *Black*, rather than *African-American*, because I was part of the generation that echoed James Brown's clarion cry: "Say It Loud–I'm Black and I'm Proud." I was part of the "Black is Beautiful" generation. (And besides, a monosyllable is so much more manageable than a cumbersome, if politically correct, euphemism.)

In 1953, my father moved our family to Detroit from Mississippi, where his forefathers had been slaves and sharecroppers, toiling in the cotton fields for generations. He made a decent living as a member of the UAW, and I went to decent schools in a middle-class Black neighborhood. My mother was a kind and gentle soul—what I remember of her—but her health was always fragile, and she died when I was eleven.

I studied hard and won a scholarship to the University of Chicago. I was the first person in my family to attend college. I majored in education and, after graduating, returned to my hometown and got a job as a high school teacher. It didn't pay a lot, but it was satisfying work. I liked to think I was contributing to the betterment of the Black community; giving my mostly-Black students knowledge of the world and all of its possibilities. Something to which they could aspire. Then everything went to hell.

The auto plants shut down, one by one. My father's pension dried up when Chrysler filed for bankruptcy and he couldn't make the payments on the house. I took that responsibility over and was able to carry us for a year or so. Then my father died and Detroit went bankrupt. My teacher's pension was gone. My neighborhood turned into a ghost town seemingly overnight, filled with empty, boarded-up houses that were falling to ruin and becoming homes to crack dealers and gang-bangers. My middle-class neighborhood was now a dangerous place. I was mugged and robbed on my own street more than once.

I continued teaching well into my sixties. But at last, they forced me to retire. I had no pension, only my meager Social Security income. I had to take a second mortgage on the house from the bank that held our first mortgage. I'll never forget the man at the bank who gave me the loan. A white man named McKinnon. He insisted that I call him Jerry. Jerry had all the oily charm of a used car salesman. He gave me a byzantine contract to sign with more fine print than the disclaimer on Humira. "Don't worry," he told me, "the housing market will bounce back soon and your house will be worth more than it was when you bought it." I knew it was a bad deal, but I didn't know just how bad until later. The interest and the payments went up and up.

I had to find a job. Any job. I went to work at the local McDonald's, dispensing burgers and fries at the drive-thru window. I worked from 4 p.m. to midnight. One night, as we were cleaning up and getting ready to close, three boys wearing ski masks came in. One of them approached Claudine, who was at the cash register. He produced a sawed-off shotgun from under his long coat and demanded she fill a bag with cash. The armored car had already come and gone, collecting most of the cash for that day. The cash register yielded exactly $27.83. The boy shot Claudine in the face. I saw her brains go flying out of the back of her head. She was just sixteen years old. The next day, I resigned from McDonald's.

My Social Security income was not as much as the house payments. I fell further and further behind. At last, my home was repossessed by the bank. By Jerry. I was now homeless.

*

Gradually it dawned on me that I was dead. I must've frozen to death on that park bench. The bench I was on bordered on a verdant park. This place — was it heaven? It certainly had a heavenly appearance, but not what I was brought up to expect. No angels, no St. Peter, no pearly gates. And where was God? Was there a God? Maybe He was in one of these palatial buildings that lined the street. And what were all these alien beings? Could heaven be the same for every creature in the universe?

There was a bright, golden star that lit the dark blue sky, but it was not the Sun and it was not an Earthly sky. Streams of glowing objects flowed to and from it. When I put on my sunglasses and squinted upward, I could see that these objects were beings of some kind. Souls? Maybe that light was God.

*

While I should have felt great joy landing in this place, I was still plagued by an abiding bitterness toward the bank, the school board, the whole system that had ruined my city and killed me. But mostly toward Jerry. I thirsted for revenge. I wanted to make his life the living hell he had made mine.

I wanted to pray for guidance. But now I doubted there would be anyone to hear my prayers. I looked up at the Hall of Knowing. I must have been placed here for a reason. I crossed the street and started climbing the steps. My old aches and pains were gone. I felt as strong and agile as I had when I was twenty. With each step, I gained more strength. At last, I reached the top and passed through the great doors, which swung open for me as I approached.

✳

Inside, aside from the high, majestic ceilings and marble walls, the place looked like nothing so much as a Las Vegas casino. It was crowded with beings operating machines that looked like slot machines. There was a chorus of strange beeping and ringing sounds, which added to the Vegas mien. Everyone was talking out loud to the machines, asking questions, and the machines were responding in their own language audibly and visually on large screens. I cautiously approached one of the machines that was not in use and seated myself on the stool before it. It made some odd sounds and the screen, evidently detecting my language was English, lit up and said: "Ask me a question and pull the lever."

"Am I dead?" (*Cha-ching!* A bell rang every time I pulled the lever.)

"Yes."

"What is this place?"

"The Hall of Knowing in the city of In Between."

"In between what and what?"

"In between your former existence and your next existence."

"Can you tell me what my next existence will be?"

"No. That will be determined by you. What you were and what you want."

"I want revenge."

"You want to go back to Detroit?"

"How do you know I'm from Detroit?"

"I know all things about you, Richard Partridge."

"How?"

"From your ass."

"I beg your pardon?"

"As soon as you parked your ass on that stool, I knew everything you had ever done, ever felt, ever wished for."

"Oh." I had to let this sink in. "So you know about Jerry, the bad loan, the park bench?"

"Of course."

"So I don't need to tell you what I want to do. How can I get back to Detroit and torment Jerry?"

"You want to be a ghost. But not just an ordinary ghost, a poltergeist. For that, you need special training. You must go to the Ghost Academy."

The Ghost Academy. It had a nice ring to it. "How do I get there?"

"Go out the front door, make a right, walk two blocks, third building on your right, opposite the carousel."

"Thank you." I started to get up.

"May I make a suggestion?"

"Okay."

"I suggest you abandon this plan and choose instead to train yourself for the Ascension."

"What's the Ascension?"

"It's where everyone winds up anyway. What you want is just a waste of time. A waste of centuries. All beings ascend sooner or later. You're just asking for another existence of turmoil and misery. You could shortcut that and go directly to Absolute Bliss and merge with The One."

"How do I find The One?"

"Just go outside and look up. You can see the Ascension and the Replenishing going on ceaselessly, as it always has and always will."

So what I thought I saw was true. The Supreme Being was that star, and those tiny drops of light were souls. I had to sit in silence for a moment and process all this. At last, I said "Thanks, but I'm going down the street to the Ghost Academy. That bastard needs to be taught a lesson." Of course, the machine had to have the last word.

"There will be lessons for everyone."

✶

The Ghost Academy was an ornate, Victorian affair. It looked like the Addams Family house from the old TV series, or maybe the home of Norman Bates and his mother in Hitchcock's *Psycho*. Apparently, they took the haunted house cliché quite literally.

I walked up the creaky wooden steps to the front porch, opened the creaky screen door, and knocked. "Enter," came a deep, scary voice from within. It reverberated through an artificial-sounding echo chamber. I entered and there, seated behind a desk in the foyer, was a short, white-haired man. The most mild-mannered, harmless-looking person one could imagine.

"Did I scare you?" he inquired, hopefully.

"A little," I said.

"Oh," said the little man, crestfallen. "How about now?" He turned a knob on a control panel on his desk and spoke loudly into a microphone: "Enter!" The reverb repeated as if bouncing off the walls of a cave.

"That was better."

"Now, what can we do for you?"

"I want to haunt someone. I want to scare the hell out of them. Maybe to death."

"Well, you've come to the right place," said the little man

gleefully. "You want to be a poltergeist. To be a ghost is one thing. Ghosts have no power over their physical environment. They just hang around. They can't be heard, seen, or affect any changes, like moving objects or turning lights on and off. A poltergeist, on the other hand, is a ghost who has developed powers to manipulate the physical world and even to make his voice heard. That's what you want, right?"

I nodded, suddenly a little unsure of what I was getting myself into.

"Well, it takes work and practice, but if you apply yourself, we can give you those powers."

"I don't have any money."

The little man laughed. "Money! We don't have money here. You'll just need to fill out a few forms." He shoved a clipboard toward me with a few pages of forms. They were like what you fill out in a doctor's office: Full name, years of birth and death, ethnicity, a history of surgeries, family illnesses, allergies, etc., etc. At the end, I had to sign a long disclaimer indemnifying the Ghost Academy of any responsibility should any harm befall me. I sat down, filled out the forms, signed the disclaimer without reading it, and handed the forms back to the little man. He picked up his telephone and muttered "A Richard Partridge to see you, Madame. New student." He hung up and looked at me. "Just have a seat, Mrs. Spector will be with you shortly."

At length, a tall, pale woman with long, white hair entered. She was dressed in a diaphanous white gown. She looked quite ghostly herself. She smiled.

"Hello, Richard." I rose and we shook hands. Her hand was icy. "I'm Mrs. Spector, the Dean of Ghost Academy. Come this way." She about-faced and I followed her down a long corridor that was adorned with dust and cobwebs, in keeping with the rest of the decor. On either side were doors with glass windows, through which I could see classes in progress. In one room, a ball was being passed through the air from student to student, without anyone touching it. The teachers and students all looked like normal, average humans of every race.

"No extraterrestrials?" I asked.

"Apparently, haunting is unique to Earthlings."

"I wonder why."

"Because haunting is motivated by one of two things: anger and revenge or the desire to stay near loved ones who are still living. These emotions are unique to Earthlings."

We entered Mrs. Spector's office. She sat behind her desk, which was cluttered with stacks of papers, and invited me to sit in the chair opposite.

"Tell me what brings you here."

I told her my story, how Jerry McKinnon of the Great Midwestern Bank had deceived me into taking a loan he knew would result in my eviction. "I don't know how he sleeps at night now, but when I get through with him he won't be sleeping at all," I concluded bitterly.

She looked at the clipboard that had the papers I had signed. "Are you aware that, once you're back in Detroit, you won't be able to come back here. You'll have to stay there as an angry spirit for at least 100 years."

"And after that?"

"After that, you will transcend to a region known as the Netherworld. It's a dark, cold place. Not nearly so nice as here. You'll have to stay there for another 800 years. At the end of that time, if your bitterness has dissipated, you get to return here and pick up right where you are now."

This gave me pause. "Hmm. Can I think about this for a day or two?"

"Yes. But I can do even better than that. I can send you as an unseen spirit to Jerry's home this minute. You won't be able to do anything and no one will know you are there, but you can observe. Then I will bring you back. If you still want to haunt him, you may begin classes."

"Send me."

※

The next thing I knew I was in Jerry's bedroom. It was late at night. In the darkness, I could hear him tossing around in his sleep, muttering and moaning. As my eyes adjusted to the darkness, I could make out three ectoplasmic men, one black, one white, and one brown, gathered around his bed, whispering things in his ears.

"You made me lose my family. They left me when you evicted us," said one.

"My little girl died of pneumonia when we couldn't get into the homeless shelter," said another.

"When you took our home, I couldn't get a job, so I killed myself. Now we're going to kill you," said the third.

At this, Jerry sat bolt upright and screamed, then turned and buried his face in the pillow and sobbed. "I'm sorry. I was only doing my job. Please, leave me in peace. You scared away my wife and kids, I've quit the bank, and now *I'm* being evicted. Isn't that enough for you?"

"No. We want you to suffer as we did. We want your soul. There's a gun in the drawer of the night table. Use it and come with us to the Netherworld. We'll show you a real good time." They all laughed ghoulishly.

I turned and walked — or rather glided — through the closed door of the bedroom, down the hall, and through the front door of the house onto the street. I looked up at the night sky of Detroit. Stars twinkled. The moon was bright. I knew this was the last I would ever see of the sky from Earth. I looked up and shouted.

"Mrs. Spector, Mrs. Spector, I've seen enough. Take me back!"

And she did.

JUST DESSERTS

I was close to my last gasp. "Is Bishop Murray coming?" I asked Brother Joseph, with unconcealed desperation.

"He said he would come."

"But when? I haven't got much time." I was barely able to wheeze out the words. I was in renal failure. My liver was shot. The doctor had said I wouldn't last the night.

I had killed my liver with booze. The booze was to kill my guilt. The guilt was from molesting sixteen little boys and little girls, between the ages of four and ten, throughout my twenty-year career as a parish priest. I knew I was headed for hell, but my last shot at redemption was to receive my last rites from someone high up in the Church, someone closer to God, someone with rank and gravitas, someone who might be able to slip a word on my behalf into the divine ear of God Himself and gain me some kind of clemency, a chance to wriggle out of the fate I knew I so richly deserved. And so, now that the time had come, I called for Bishop Murray.

Bishop Murray was not unaware of my shenanigans. He had received many complaints about me from mortified parents, and some even from children who had reached adulthood and could no longer conceal the shame and hatred I had engendered in them. And, each time, Bishop Murray had discretely reassigned me to another parish. But, six years ago, when all the scandals about predatory priests started erupting everywhere, and when one of my victims hanged himself, leaving a graphic note detailing my abuses, Bishop Murray packed me off to a retirement home in the country, where I was able to quietly drink myself to death. My victim's suicide note was never shown to the authorities. In return, the victim was buried in consecrated ground, ignoring the rule about suicides not being given this privilege.

My name is Father Kevin Flaherty, late of the parish of Dorchester, Massachusetts, and I am a child molester. But surely Bishop Murray can pull some strings...

At last, he arrived. I was beginning to hallucinate, perhaps from the ever-increasing dosage of morphine coming through the tube they had inserted into my vein. The ceiling of my modest room was now painted with apparitions, little children, angry angels, my victims. Bishop Murray sat on my bed and made the sign of the cross. He anointed my forehead with chrism. We recited the Our Father together:

> Our Father, who art in heaven,
> hallowed be thy name.
> Thy kingdom come.
> Thy will be done
> on earth, as it is in heaven.

On earth, as it is in heaven. If that is true, wouldn't it follow that the reverse would be true? *In heaven, as it is on earth*? So there might be some hope for me. If the same corruption that riddled the Catholic Church on earth also prevailed in heaven, I had a chance. He then asked me if I was "heartily sorry for my sins."

"Oh, yes, Father. Yes, yes, yes. Heartily, heartily sorry."

"Let's not overdo it, Kevin," said Bishop Murray.

"Say five Hail Marys, and you will be absolved of your sins," he said.

Only five? Given the weight of my sins, I would have thought I'd be saying Hail Marys to my last breath, which was to come all too soon. But I said them as loudly and fervently as my failing breath would allow.

"I absolve you of your earthly sins, in the name of the Father, and of the Son, and of the Holy Spirit. Amen."

"Amen," I wheezed with my last breath.

※

When I awoke I was looking up at a beautiful blue sky. I was lying in a vast meadow of the greenest grass, dotted with wildflowers. The sun was shining brightly. A gentle breeze caressed my skin. I was young again! I sat up and rubbed my eyes. As far as my eyes could see, there was nothing but green grass, a few trees, and wildflowers. *Could this be true? Had I really dodged the bullet? I had made it to the Elysian Fields. Bishop Murray really had some pull.*

Off in the distance, I could see two little structures. As I drew closer, I could see the first was an orange crate, manned by a towheaded little boy, no more than five. It had a sign: LEMONADE 5¢. As I got closer, I could see the boy was completely naked. Was this a trick of the Devil to tempt me? The little boy smiled at me. "Want a lemonade, mister?"

"I would love a lemonade, little boy." Then I noticed I was wearing the night shirt I had been wearing when I died. No pockets. "Sorry," I said, shrugging, "it seems I have no money."

"Oh, that's okay. You can pay later." He scooped up some ice cold lemonade with a ladle, poured it into a paper cup, and handed it to me.

"Oh, bless you, my child. I was very thirsty." The lemonade was delicious. All the while I was eyeing the little boy. He was flawless: blond, chubby, a wingless cherub. Just my type. Then I realized the bulge of my erection was starting to show through my night shirt.

"What's that?" he asked innocently, pointing to it.

"Oh, that. That just means I'm happy to see you. Are there more little boys and girls here?"

"Oh yes." He pointed to another wooden structure, a hundred yards further on. I thanked him and told him I would pay him his nickel as soon as I could find someone to provide me with some money and some clothes. I set off toward the little structure. As I got closer, I saw that it was a stand with a sign overhead that read JUST DESSERTS. Behind the counter was a naked little girl, almost a cookie-cutter copy of the little boy at the lemonade stand. On the counter were all kinds of lovely confections: cupcakes, eclairs, various candies and — could those be charlotte russes?

"You like charlotte russes, mister?" asked the little girl.

"Oh yes. I haven't seen these since I was a little child myself."

"Have one," said the child.

"But I have no money, my child." I showed her the pocketless nightshirt I was wearing.

"Oh, that's okay. Money isn't that important here," she said.

I took one. It was wrapped in a white cardboard cup, just as I remembered, and there was whipped cream and a maraschino cherry on top. As you consumed the cake-and-custard filling, you pushed up on the cardboard bottom of the cup to bring out more layers of deliciousness. It was the best thing I had eaten in sixty years. "God bless you, my child," I said. "This is wonderful. Are there more children around here?" I asked.

She pointed to a grove of trees several hundred yards on. "Oh yes. They're all over there, playing."

I started off toward the grove. As I drew nearer, I could hear the sound of little voices singing. "Ring around the rosie, a pocket full of posies, ashes, ashes, we all fall *down*!"

When I reached the grove I could see through the trees a circular clearing, with shafts of sunlight pouring down. The little children — boys and girls — were hand in hand, forming a circle. They were much like the boy selling lemonade and the girl selling desserts: all blond, no more than five years old, and stark naked. My boner grew. I focused my thoughts on the Lord's Prayer to make it go down. When it had shrunk sufficiently for me to show myself, I entered the clearing.

"Hello, boys and girls," I called, sounding as cheerful and benevolent as possible. "Do any of you know where I can find some clothes? Are there any grownups here?"

"I am here," came a deep voice from the shade of a large oak.

I walked toward the sound of the voice. A tall, elegant man of perhaps forty was seated on a canvas-and-wood folding chair, the kind people used to take to the beach when I was a child myself. He was dressed all in black. Then I saw the priest's collar. I approached him, trying to decipher what the half-smile on his face could mean.

"Good afternoon, Father. It's good to see a brother of the cloth. I've just arrived here. Can you tell me where I am?"

"I'm afraid not, Father Flaherty," he said. "That's something you'll have to find out for yourself."

I gave him a puzzled look. "Well, then, can you get me some clothes—like yours?"

"Very well." He gave a slight wave of his hand, and suddenly I was fully clothed in my clerical collar and black attire.

"Thank you. And, if I may, could I borrow some small change?" I chuckled with embarrassment. "You see, a dear little boy back there gave me a glass of lemonade on credit. And then there was a little girl, selling desserts."

"Yes, 'Just Desserts.' Don't worry about the money," he said. "I'll take care of it."

"Thank you, Father, but I feel I should go back there and give it to them personally."

"Why?" asked the priest. "There are plenty more little boys and girls right here for you to play with." He smiled, a leering, menacing smile. "And they're all naked. Just the way you like them, isn't that so? I can see your boner right through your raiment."

I felt the hairs on my neck stand up and fear began to churn in my belly.

"Children," called the priest, "come, let's show Father Flaherty what we're playing. Right this way, Father Flaherty." And, with that, he rose. He was very tall, very imposing.

"You're not really a priest, are you?"

"Well, no. I thought it would reassure you. Would you like to see what I really am?"

"I think I can guess."

"I'll show myself in a way you'll probably understand better." And suddenly, before me stood the Devil, Lucifer, Satan Himself: all fiery-red, with horns, a tail that ended in a barbed point, and cloven hooves. I wanted to run, but somehow had to follow him. He led me to the circle where the children were playing. They parted to let us enter. On the ground lay a wooden cross, big and old enough to be the very one used to crucify our Lord. And next to that was a large, round pit. I approached it and looked down. It seemed to have no bottom, but, far down in the distance, there was a fiery glow. There was a rope attached to the bottom of the cross, which ran through a pulley that was attached to a sturdy bough of the oak tree, high above. Then it led down to a winch that had yards and yards of rope coiled around it and a big crank. Now I knew what they were going to do.

As one, the children swarmed all over me, knocked me to the ground and carried me to the cross. They tied me onto it and ripped off my shoes. Then they started hammering spikes through my feet. I screamed in pain. I had no idea anything could hurt so much and still stay conscious.

"Hurts, doesn't it?" said Lucifer. "Well, this is nothing compared to the pain you caused all those children and their families."

"But I said I was sorry. Heartily sorry. I received absolution from Bishop Murray himself," I screamed.

"Yes, well, don't worry. We'll be receiving him as well. In the near future," said Lucifer.

Blood was spurting from my feet. Then they started on my wrists.

When I was fully tied up and nailed down, they all pitched in to turn the crank on the winch. My cross was lifted from the bottom, high in the air, until I was suspended, upside down, right above the bottomless pit.

"You priests make me laugh," said Lucifer. "You've got your pathetic, superstitious parishioners convinced that you are somehow endowed with Divine authority and, filled with the arrogance and pride that only comes with the illusion of power, you con your followers into believing that, if they do as you say, they will go to heaven. And, if they don't, they will go to hell. You even had yourself convinced, didn't you, Father? Well, now you see how it really works and, Father Flaherty, you can go straight to *hell*." And, with that, he cut the rope and I plummeted downward, screaming "Noooooooooo!" until I ran out of breath. And still, there was no bottom in sight.

MONSTER ZOO

Call me Jake. About a month ago—as near as I can guess—I died of Leukemia at the age of twelve. As a child, I was always sickly and never really got to have any fun. When I woke up in that beautiful city, I was in a special place set aside for kids. There were kindly adults there called guides, some of them from my planet, Earth, and some from other planets—even other galaxies—whose task it was to show us around and make sure we felt safe in the city of In Between. Personally, I felt great; never better. I got to hang with other kids, everybody was nice and friendly, and I could run, jump, and play all kinds of sports like I never could when I was alive.

Each of us had a personal guide who watched over us. Mine was Burdok. He was an Archronesian, from the planet Archronis in the Triangulum Galaxy, which his people called Lorf. Burdok and I could talk without sound. We could read each other's thoughts. Not private thoughts, just when we wanted to communicate. He looked kind of like a person, but his skin was dark red, his eyes were violet and had lids that opened and closed from the sides. His hair looked like a punk rock mohawk, standing straight up right down the middle of his skull and he had a tail with a third hand. Once, as he picked a fruit from the Gabok tree, the sweetest, juiciest fruit in the known universe, he quipped: "Sometimes a tail really comes in handy." I was amazed at his ability to master the English language so quickly as to make a pun. I guess I've just described a punk-rock devil, but Burdok didn't look like a devil at all. He was my guardian angel. He told me lots of cool stories about life on his planet. The Archronesians are a race of storytellers, it's just in their nature.

*

One day, we all went on a field trip to the zoo of In Between. Now, in the city of In Between, most animals are allowed to roam free, since they don't want to harm anyone. Even lions and tigers don't harm anyone because they're not hungry. Nobody needs to eat here. But in the zoo, they keep the dangerous animals, the ones that are so wild and vicious they'd tear anyone apart, even though we're all dead already. These monsters are called *soul-eaters*. They can literally devour someone's soul, which would prevent them from Ascending.

We had all been taught about the Ascension and the Replenishing the first day we got here. We could look up any time we wanted and see it going on all the time. The golden star in the dark blue sky was The One, the Creator of the Universe, and you could see all the old souls, like tiny droplets of light, ascending and merging with The One, and all the new souls streaming out of The One at the same time to find homes in new bodies that were being born all over the Universe. This was called the Replenishing. It would happen to us all sooner or later. It's so simple, the way it works, it's a wonder no one on Earth was ever able to figure it out in all the centuries of thinking.

But if a soul-eater gets you, that's it. It's really the end. The only end possible, I suppose.

*

At the zoo, there they were: the most fearsome creatures in all creation. There were many different species of soul-eater, and there was one example of each encased in a large cube of something that looked like clear plastic. They did not suffocate and they did not starve, even though there was no way to feed them in there. And who would want to feed them his soul, anyway? One species looked kind of like a reptile or maybe a carnivorous dinosaur, with scaly skin, a row of sharp points on its back, terrifying claws and teeth, and bolts of lightning shooting out of its eyes. Another one looked like a giant insect, a cross between a spider and a praying mantis, with a million eyes within its eyes, like a fly. They thrashed around angrily inside their cubicles and made sounds that were so terrifying, I can't even describe them.

Every few feet along the path there were tall metal boxes with glass windows, like the way they store fire extinguishers on Earth. Inside the boxes were long things that looked like spears, and each had a sign: IN CASE OF EMERGENCY, BREAK GLASS and there was a metal thing on a chain to break the glass.

"There are thousands more of each variety," said Burdok pointing to the soul-eaters, "but they are sequestered on another world, from which they cannot escape."

"So, these things are all dead, like us?" I asked.

"Yes," said Burdok, "but on my world, there are live ones. The ones we have on Archronis are called Rragosti. They are kept at bay by a brave group of Archronesians called the Molki. The Molki patrol outside the walls of each city and slay the Rragosti with Krajungs—*lightning spears*." He indicated the spears in the tall metal boxes. "And often, the Molka loses the fight and is devoured, soul and all."

✻

Burdok led me through the maze of cubes to the scariest beast of all. "This is a Rragosta. The name comes from the sound they make." And, as if on cue, the thing looked at us and let out a creepy noise that sort of sounded like *rraaaa!* It wasn't a loud sound, more like a terrible whisper, right in your ear. It was the scariest sound I ever heard. When it saw Burdok, it was like it recognized him. It started to throw itself against the walls of its cell with such force, the whole cube started to rock off its foundations. People started screaming and running in all directions. I could see cracks begin to form in the cube. Burdok turned to me. "Run," he said. But I stood rooted to the spot, too scared—and fascinated—to move. At last, the cube came apart and the creature came forth, like a newborn bird out of its egg. Burdok turned and pointed at the spear box. I was standing right next to it. I broke the glass and tossed the spear to him, just as the beast was about to devour him, whispering its horrible scream. Burdok grabbed the Krajung. Electricity crackled from its tip. As the monster devoured Burdok, he thrust the point of the weapon through the throat of the creature—from the inside. The last sound I heard was the voice of Burdok inside the beast: "Molkiiii!" He'd killed the monster, but not before it killed him.

※

When I think of Burdok's heroism, I realize the enormity of his sacrifice. To save me and everyone around us, Burdok had committed himself to the most horrible fate imaginable. Can you imagine nothingness? It's like sleep with no dreams. It's the thing human beings fear more than anything. Burdok accepted this fate: eternal *nothingness*.

※

Burdok will live on in my memory, even as I glide through the ether toward The One, a droplet of golden light.

PERCHANCE TO DREAM

It must have been the fever. Strange visions haunted my dreams; visions of angels and devils, all beckoning me to join them. They offered me splendid rewards if I went to their side. The angels offered me eternal peace and light, a bed of clouds, no more work, just beautiful music and singing in praise of the Almighty for the rest of time. The devils — and there were some pretty sexy ones — offered me wild orgies, endless hedonistic parties, I could eat all I wanted and anything I wanted, I could take any drugs, drink myself silly, and never suffer any consequences, never age, never be sick.

When I awoke, I was soaked in sweat. I became more delirious with each passing day. It was an occupational hazard. If you choose to serve as a Christian missionary in the Solomon Islands where malaria is rampant, this is the chance you take. Quinine was the only treatment, but we had none. It was January 1942. The Japanese had invaded many of the Solomon Islands but bypassed Sikaiana, the tiny atoll where I was the only white man. There was no navigable harbor there and it was treacherous to all but the native canoes because of the coral reefs. Still, they had cut off all our supply routes, and we couldn't get any food or medicine. There were thirty other people on the island who were also dying of malaria, almost a tenth of the entire population.

*

I had converted all the natives — all 340 of them — to Christianity, to my church, the Anglican Church. In the two years I had spent on Sikaiana, we had built a small church. I had furnished bibles to all the inhabitants. Every Sunday, everyone would congregate at the church and I would preach a sermon. A lot of my sermons had to do with avoiding the temptations of the flesh. You see, the Polynesian people are natural hedonists. Left to their own devices, they would be having big parties, roasting wild pigs in pits covered with palm leaves, beating on drums, and dancing lewd, suggestive dances. And then making mad, passionate love all over the place. I taught them that this was not the will of God; not the will of Jesus Christ, our Savior.

It took a lot of sermonizing and some private arm-twisting with the local king and his elders, but, after two years, I believe I was pretty successful in suppressing the natural instincts of these primitive people. The regular shipments of rice, beans, and canned vegetables from the Church didn't hurt either.

✻

After many days of delirium dreams, one night, I fell asleep and had a very different kind of dream...

✻

I awoke in a majestic hall, with spiral columns supporting arched muqarnas, squinches and a vaulted dome in the center of the square of columns and arches. It looked like a Moorish palace. It was cool and silent and I felt a great peace come over me.

A bearded man with long dark hair and robes entered. He was swarthy and looked to be from the Middle East. He called me by my name.

"Ethan Morley. Sit," he said, indicating a cushion on the floor at a large round table inlaid with beautiful mosaic tiles. He had the air of kingly authority and he did not look pleased to see me. He sat on a cushion opposite me. "Do you know where you are?"

"No." I was no longer calm. I remembered the ague of the malaria and now I was on the verge of a terrible realization. It was not only that I was dead, but that my life had been a waste of time. "Wh-who are you?" I stuttered.

"I think you know."

I don't know how I knew, but I did know. I was sitting opposite Jesus Christ. "My Lord," I said, prostrating myself on the spotless floor.

"Get up. There's no bowing and scraping around here. I've seen so many of you so-called Christians come through here. I don't know why they make me interview every one of you. You're all dead; you cannot go back and change things."

"What would you have me change?"

"I would have you go back and tell all the deluded leaders of your religion—and all the other religions—that they have perverted my teachings. I never wanted a religion in my name. I never wanted to be worshipped. I just wanted people to love each other and stop fighting. Instead, you fight under my banner. You start wars in my name. You tell everybody who does not believe as you do that they better change their minds or be damned for all eternity. Many of you really believe this, but worse are the ones who just use it cynically to further their own ends."

I was dumbstruck. "You mean, everything I've been preaching to my flock is wrong?"

"Of course it's wrong, you ninny!"

"But, what was I to say to them?"

"You shouldn't have been there in the first place. They were better off without you and your sermonizing... If you had to teach them anything, it's this: Stop hating. All men are your brothers. Stop fighting and killing. God is love and love, in all its forms, is good. Everything that's natural to man and doesn't hurt anyone else is fine."

I sat in silence for a long time. I thought hard about my life, how wrong I had been about so many things.

"What if I could go back? Can you fix it so I can?"

Jesus had a good laugh at this. "What if I could? What would you do? Look what they did to me. Are you going to stop the war singlehandedly? Going to have a talk with Herr Hitler? Tojo? Mussolini? Are you going to tell them Jesus sent you down from heaven?" He laughed some more, then we were both silent.

"So what happens now? Am I in heaven?"

"Yes, if that's what you want to call it. It's not forever, but while you're here, you can continue to learn. You can evolve. Then, when you're ready, you go back to earth and are born again, a better, wiser person than you were the last time. I learned about this system — reincarnation it's called — when I was in India. I taught it to my followers, the men you call apostles. They all believed in this, but years later, when men started this church in my name, they made up different myths that made it easier for them to control their followers. They made up heaven and hell. If you did what they said, you'd go to heaven for all eternity. If not, you would be condemned to eternal fire in hell. But that's not the way it works at all."

"Is there no punishment for the wicked, then?"

"Oh, there is. It's called karma. If you do evil in this life, you suffer in the next, or maybe in five lifetimes. No one knows the mind of The One."

✻

Of course, I knew this was all a dream and I would soon wake up. In a way, I did. I stayed in that place — In Between it was called — for 100 years, as near as I can figure. I learned many things. I meditated. I evolved. I learned that I would be born again on earth in the year 2042, I would be a strong, wise person, but I would remember none of this.

PRISONERS

My name is Simon LeConte. You might think I'm French with a name like that, but I'm an American. My family has lived in western Maine, near the Kennebec River, going back five centuries, which, before there was a United States, was Acadia, a province of French Canada.

I can't say I lived a happy life; I had some bad breaks. After losing my job at the Kimberly-Clark paper mill, I took to drinking heavily. To be honest, I was drinking before I lost my job. In fact, that's *why* I lost my job. My wife, Vivian, a mean and spiteful woman, who is the one who drove me to drink in the first place, divorced me and took what little money I had left. She also took my only child, my daughter, Oxana, who is now sixteen. She took my house, where my family had lived for generations. When I got the eviction notice, I hung myself from a beam in my garage. My idea was to never leave that house, to stay and haunt Vivian forever. But that's not the way it worked out.

I found myself in a dark, damp place, a special purgatory just for suicides. For a long time, I wandered those moldy corridors, sometimes passing another lost soul, but never speaking to anyone. Every once in a while, I thought I could hear voices from far, far away, from the land of the living. Usually, these were distressed souls crying out for help. I wanted to help them, but what could I do? I was trapped there and no one in the living world could hear me.

Oxana is the child of my first marriage. Her mother,

Mariana, was beautiful and kind. She died of a cerebral hemorrhage when Oxana was only three. I think I died then too.

Now Vivian had Oxana in her clutches. She kept her a virtual prisoner. She took her to school, picked her up at the end of the day, and drove her straight home. Oxana was not allowed to have friends visit, was not allowed to go out. How did I know this? When I was still, when I sat in a corner and closed my eyes, I could see what Oxana saw, feel what she felt. She just sat in her room and cried. Sometimes I would pray to Mariana to help me help our daughter.

One day I saw Oxana eyeing the razor blades in the medicine cabinet. Another time, she took a long, sharp knife from the kitchen and hid it under her mattress. It seemed clear that Vivian would drive Oxana to suicide just like she did me — unless I could stop her. Even if I couldn't really do anything to change things for Oxana, maybe I could convince her to hang on for another couple of years. Then she'd be old enough to get away on her own. And I could tell her the terrible fate that would await her if she killed herself.

Those endless corridors were lined with doors. As I wandered, never passing the same way twice, I tried each door, but they were always locked. Each doorknob was unique: some plain, some ornate. Some looked to be hundreds of years old. I wondered: *what's behind these doors; why are they here?*

One day I came to a door with daylight seeping through the cracks. All this time I thought I was far underground, and now this. What did it mean? I looked in either direction. There was no one around. I turned the knob, and the door opened onto — *sky*. It was wonderful to feel the fresh, clean wind blowing hard on my face, through my hair. I looked down thousands of feet and saw only clouds. I looked up and saw only endless blue. What is this? Could the myths of heaven be literally true? If I jumped, what would happen? Was this an invitation to a second suicide? Could one die twice? I wanted to jump, but I was afraid. I've always had a fear of heights, but what could be worse than endlessly wandering these sodden halls? I had to think. I closed the door and sat on the floor. Maybe this was a sign from Mariana, an answer to my prayers. Maybe, if I took the leap, it would somehow help Oxana. I opened the door, closed my eyes, and jumped.

As I fell, I screamed. I screamed my daughter's name. "Oxaaanaaaaaa!" I felt myself plummeting downward. I plummeted for a long time. I was spinning and it was making me ill. Finally, I opened my eyes and looked down. That carpet of clouds below seemed as distant as when I first opened the door. Then, I spread my arms and legs, like a skydiver, eyes open wide. I was flying! So beautiful...

Soon, out of the corner of my eye, I saw another skydiver next to me. It was Mariana! We turned to each other and smiled. She reached out her hand. As soon as my hand touched hers, the scene changed abruptly.

We were in my daughter's room, sitting on her bed. Mariana looked as angelic as I imagined she would, having lived a virtuous life. Oxana was sitting between us, but she didn't know we were there. It was night, and Oxana was getting ready for bed.

"We have to wait until she's asleep," said Mariana. "Then we can talk to her."

We got up as Oxana got into bed. Soon she was asleep.

"Mariana," I whispered, "will I have to go back to the purgatory I was in? Couldn't I stay here with you?"

"No," whispered Mariana, "you will have to go back when we have accomplished what we came here to do."

"Oh," I said. Disappointment is not a strong enough word for what I felt. Then she whispered in Oxana's ear.

"Oxana," said Mariana, "it's Mommy and Daddy. We're here with you."

"Mommy... Daddy?" Oxana mumbled in her sleep.

"Listen, Oxana, this is your Daddy. I saw that you were thinking of killing yourself. I came to tell you not to. I did it and I was sent to a horrible place, a place I will always inhabit. It's dark and damp, and…"

Oxana opened her eyes and sat bolt upright. "Killing myself? I wasn't going to kill myself. I was going to kill Vivian."

THE WAITING ROOM

The waiting room was cold and damp. The light was poor, but you were expected to fill out your application, hand it in, then wait. I had nothing but the suit I was buried in. If I had been able to dress myself, I would have had my good pen. But no one thinks to put a pen in your pocket when you're dead. So the clerk, a stick-thin man of about forty with greasy hair, gave me a cheap ballpoint that wrote in light blue ink and skipped. They sat you at an old-fashioned child's desk. The kind you had in elementary school, with the writing tray attached to the chair, and all scratched up, making it almost impossible to write neatly.

I was not alone in that dreary room. I could vaguely make out, out of the corners of my eyes, other souls hunched over their little desks, writing feverishly. But they were not in clear focus. A smoky haze seemed to permeate everything.

Filling out the form was long and painstaking: place of birth, date of birth, date of death, every institution of learning attended, any special achievements or distinctions at school, every job, promotions, reasons for leaving...

Then there was the essay section, in which you were able to make the case for your admission to heaven. Good and selfless acts, how you made the world a better place. I had a lot of trouble with this section. It was hard for me to remember any special things I had done that were especially good — or bad.

One rainy night I rescued a stray dog and brought it home. But we had to bring it to the pound a few days later when it bit one of the kids. I guess they killed it.

I wrote about the many injustices to which I had been subjected. Honors at school and at work that should have been mine, but always went to someone else. How I had offered, out of the goodness of my heart, to share the driveway that was my designated parking spot with my new neighbor, a blonde girl from New England. And how she had then conspired with my landlord to get me evicted from my parking space, and how my car was relegated to the street. But I did not lash out. I choked back my rage. I maintained my composure. She remained my neighbor, her car occupying the parking space she had stolen, for ten long years. And I was always civil. I never said a bad word. Surely, that was a good deed.

I told how I had married. I was at the lowest ebb of my life at the time. Annie was a rather plain girl—very different from the flashy Hollywood types I had always gone with—but she was stable and intelligent. She had a rent-controlled apartment and a good paying job. I had bottomed out on cocaine and alcohol and had no visible means of support. Annie got me back on my feet. She provided a safe haven and helped me start a career in the music business. We had two children, a boy and a girl, in the space of less than two years.

Then I fell in love. She was someone I'd met through mutual friends. We both fell madly, passionately in love. But we were both married. I had two little children and she had a very rich husband. He had been her childhood sweetheart. There was no sex between them, but he was her devoted protector and provider. She was incapable of finding an ordinary job. She was thirty-five and had never had to earn a living in her life. And besides, she would never leave her best friend.

And so we deemed our love impossible.

Many years later, after my children had grown up and I had long been divorced from Annie, we reconnected. Her rich husband was dead, I had no wife, my children were no longer an obligation, and we still loved each other. She told me there had never been anyone but me. I told her she was the only love of my life. And still, she would not see me. She was inconsolable after the loss of her husband. She had lost her rudder. She was now surrounded by people designated by him to protect her. She was a prisoner in her own home; a prisoner of her newly-acquired wealth. We spoke often on the phone, and she always promised we would see each other soon—next week. This went on for four years. We never saw each other again. I died thinking I would see her next week.

At the bottom of the form was an affidavit I had to sign, swearing by Almighty God that all statements made were true and accurate. I signed and handed the form in to the clerk at the window. He stamped it and told me to take a seat and wait. In the haze, I sensed others also sitting and waiting. So I waited. And waited.

In death, time does not mean the same thing as in life. I waited for what, in the land of the living, would amount to about six months. Then, one day, the clerk called my name. Doing my best to suppress my excitement, I approached the window, and was handed a letter:

> Dear (my name was filled in on a blank line),
>
> Thank you for your application. As much as we would like to send each applicant a personal response, we get so many applications, it is impossible to answer each one individually. We regret that your qualifications are not a good fit for heaven at this time. You are invited to re-apply during our next submission period, which starts at a time that will be filled in by the Waiting Room Clerk. In the meantime, you are free to apply to either hell or purgatory, whichever you feel yourself most qualified for.
>
> Best of luck,
> The Heaven Team

When I approached the window, I saw that others had received similar letters, and so I took my place in line. When I got to the front of the line, I cleared my throat and asked the clerk: "Hell is worse than purgatory, right?"

"To be sure," he said.

"Then, may I have an application for purgatory?"

The clerk smiled condescendingly. "Where do you think you are?"

BOOK II

✻

INTRODUCTION

Book II is not quite a novella, but too long to be called a short story. Like the earlier stories, it is speculative fiction, and told as a first-person narrative. But it is not about the afterlife. It's about dreams. Or should I say one long dream, dreamt in segments. A serialized dream, and as the title infers, it's in black and white.

Our narrator, an aging writer, leads a double life—his waking life and his sleeping life. He is a fan of the old black and white movies, mostly the ones made in the '40s, especially film noir. And one night he is thrust into one. In his waking life he is drab and repetitious, but in his black-and-white chiaroscuro dreamlife he is young and strong and handsome.

Ted Myers
Santa Monica, February 2023

I DREAM IN BLACK AND WHITE

It's eleven in the morning and I still don't want to wake up. I don't want to tear myself away from the dream, but already it's beginning to recede. My shoulders hurt the way they always do when I try to stay in bed too long. But why get up? What is there to look forward to? The earlier I get up, the longer the day, and I want it to be night. It's the same thing every day since I retired from the ad agency. I'd been working as a copywriter, but I was sick of writing the pap demanded by my clients. I wanted to create real literature. So I retired. But I haven't had one solid idea, either for a book, or even a short story, in two years.

I get the spam out of my email box, do a few floor exercises: stretches for my bad back, my bum knees, my torn rotator cuffs, the aches and pains that come with age. I do my truncated ten-minute yoga-breathing, mantra-saying meditation. I eat the same cereal with blueberries for breakfast. Then, the high point of my day: the bike ride. The same six-mile circuit every day, as long as the weather is nice — and, in Santa Monica, California, the weather is almost always nice. Thaw something for dinner, maybe do a little reading. Is it late enough to start drinking? At first it was five, then four, now 3:45 is acceptable for drink one: brandy and soda. Then make dinner, eat, a few more drinks — straight brandy this time — and try to zombie myself to sleep with TV. Old movies, especially the black and white ones, are my favorites. But it seems like I've seen them all. At last, after five drinks, a ten-milligram Valium, and a melatonin, I start to get drowsy. I can't wait to see what happens tonight...

※

It's always the same dream, or, more precisely, a continuation of the same movie. It's more movielike than dreamlike. There are none of the symbolic images, the non sequiturs, the people from my past who really represent someone else, the maze-like houses, trains, landscapes, and roads that used to populate my dreams. This is a completely linear movie, with a plot and characters who remain consistently themselves throughout. And it's in black and white. It's not like any dream I've ever had.

※

I'm driving my brand new 1941 Plymouth coupe fast through rainy streets. I think it's LA. I'm running away from someone. The cops? People who want to kill me? I can't remember. The answers are in last night's dream, and the night before. But I can't remember. All I know is, I've been dreaming one long film noir for—I don't know—weeks? Months?

The car skids on the slick pavement as I round a turn. I take a quick right onto La Brea, up past Hollywood Boulevard, another quick right onto Franklin. In my rearview I see a set of lights that have been following me since I left the house. I go two blocks and make a quick left onto Outpost. I'm headed up Outpost and those lights are still behind me. They disappear around a curve and I take a quick right onto a little side street, Senalda Road, and turn my lights off. The big Packard speeds past. I think I've lost them. Am I supposed to meet someone? Yes, I think that's it. A rendezvous of some kind. Now it starts to come back to me...

*

I had been contacted by a beautiful blond, Adeline Keys (played by a very young Lana Turner), to turn over some film I had taken of her wearing a certain necklace. I'm a freelance photographer and I usually sell my stuff to the *L. A. Star*, a local gossip rag. She was ready to pay me not to give the shots to the *Star*—or anyone else.

It was a family heirloom, she said. It had belonged to her mother, who had died when she was quite young. Adeline's father, Montgomery Keys, had been a politically influential financier, a man who, while he never held office, controlled the men in city hall and even the state capital in his prime. He was already old when Adeline was born. He often wondered if she was really his. Now he was a reclusive invalid—never saw or spoke to anyone except his daughter and Jerome, his trusted manservant. He didn't leave his inner sanctum, a huge, cluttered, chaotic mess of a room which composed most of the second floor of the east wing of the Keys mansion. He spent his days drinking and mumbling to himself. Adeline was beginning to worry she might have to have the old man put away.

Jerome had occupied a little room next to Keys' for thirty years. He was a small, Afro-Jamaican man of about sixty —although he looked much older—who spoke the King's English and had a weakness for Jamaican rum and opium. Keys (played by John Barrymore) was an alcoholic himself and, as long as Jerome brought him his gin and lime, and an occasional meal, Keys was satisfied. More than satisfied. He had a genuine affection for Jerome, enjoyed his witty conversation. It was hardly your typical master-servant relationship. The two would spend hours telling wild stories and cackling like a pair of lunatics. Jerome even got Keys to smoke opium with him. Keys liked that it made his legs stop hurting, but then it put him to sleep, and he didn't like that. "I'll sleep when I'm dead," he said and refused the stuff after that. In point of fact, aside from Adeline, Jerome was Keys' closest friend and confidant.

Albert, Keys' son by his first wife, occupied the west wing, along with the cook, butler, and a couple of maids. Although Keys had disowned him, Adeline had let him move back into the family estate out of pity. He was broke, having gone through all the money he'd embezzled from his father, and devoid of any employable skills. If the old man found out he was living there, he would surely have Albert thrown out of the house. But the old man never left his lair, so Adeline swore everyone to secrecy and let Albert stay. She didn't like him and she didn't trust him, but he was, after all, her half-brother. Albert knew Keys had written him out of his will, that when the old man kicked, everything would go to Adeline—if Adeline was alive.

The necklace, twelve inches of flawless emeralds set in antique twenty-four karat gold, was kept locked in a wall safe, hidden behind a painting in the old man's bedroom. There was also a big ostentatious safe in plain view. But it was a decoy filled with a lot of worthless papers. Adeline had been expressly forbidden by her father to ever wear the necklace, show it to anyone, or even mention its existence. The only reason she knew about it was that she was the only one entrusted with the safe's location and combination, in case anything happened to Keys. His will was in there too. Adeline knew the dark secret surrounding the necklace, but she was young and wild and couldn't resist wearing it to the Governor's Ball, just this once. It had all happened so long ago, surely no one would remember. So, late the night before the ball when her father was heavily drugged and snoring his head off, she sneaked into his room and opened the safe. Each time she saw it, the necklace took her breath away. The next evening, she stashed it in her gold mesh reticule.

Her date, Reggie Storrow, a rich, self-absorbed fop, arrived in his limo, right on time as always. Adeline cared nothing about him. Reggie was equally devoid of feeling but was always happy to be seen in all the right places with Adeline. Reggie and Adeline shared another dark secret, one that I knew nothing about until much later.

Once in the back seat of the limo, she put on the necklace.

"Wow, that's some sparkler," remarked Reggie.

"Just paste," said Adeline casually.

She hadn't thought about the gaggle of photographers who'd be waiting as the limos pulled up in front of the Wadsworth mansion, one of those pretentious behemoths in Hancock Park. As soon as Reggie's chauffeur opened her door and Adeline stepped out, I was Johnny-on-the-spot. I snapped a beautiful shot of her and the mysterious necklace. *What a dish*, I thought. She was dazzling in her floor-length silver satin gown that clung to her curves like a second skin. She immediately retreated back into the car as the other paparazzi snapped away, removed the necklace, stashed it in her purse, hastily scribbled a note, and entered the party on Reggie's arm, smiling as though nothing had happened. I was the only one with a shot of the necklace. As she and Reggie entered the ball, Reggie's chauffeur, a massive Black man, silent and expressionless, walked up to me and handed me the note:

> Urgent you call me. Regent 5-096. Do not print that photo. I'll make it worth your while.

It was simply signed "A". The chauffeur eyed my press badge as I read the note.

I snapped a few other celebrities that night, then packed up and went home. Out of the corner of my eye I spotted a guy in the crowd who didn't quite fit the picture. He wore a long coat and a gray fedora. He wasn't snapping pictures, and he didn't look like a celebrity hound; he looked like a thug and he was certainly eyeing me. I got in my car and beat it out of there.

My phone was ringing as I walked in the door.

"Mr. Holden?"

In the dream my name is Larry Holden. I'm twenty-six, six-feet, one-inch tall; I have wavy brown hair and a good face. I'm strong and healthy. I'm the only one in the dream not played by a recognizable actor. I'm me, the dreamer. Only my name and physical appearance are different.

"Yes?"

"No need to call me," she said. "I found you."

"Miss Keys?"

"Yes. Are you the only person that got a picture of me wearing that necklace?"

"Yes, I think so."

"Did you get my note?"

"Yes."

"I'll give you $5,000 for the undeveloped roll of film." A moment of stunned silence on my end. "Do we have a deal?"

"Am I in some kind of danger?"

"Not if you follow my instructions. Do we have a deal?"

"Five grand, cash?"

"Yes."

"All right."

"Now listen carefully. Meet me in an hour at Mulholland and Pacific View Drive. Can you find that?"

"Yeah."

"Bring the film from tonight. I'll need to see that no prints were made of that photo."

"Okay."

"And I'll bring the cash. One hour from now makes it 1 a.m. Be there."

She hung up. I lingered with the phone to my ear a moment longer. I heard a second click. Somebody else had been listening.

*

I wound my way up Outpost slowly, wanting to put as much distance as possible between me and the Packard that had been tailing me. I took a left on Mulholland when I reached the top. It was about 1,800 feet to Pacific View Drive, which zig-zagged off to the right. The rain had stopped and the landscape was illuminated by a bright full moon. I turned off my lights and parked on Mulholland a hundred feet from Pacific View. I decided to walk from there. If that Packard and whoever was in it were lying in wait for me, I wanted to see them before they saw me. I had the exposed roll of film hidden in the trunk of my car. After hearing that second click over the phone, I knew someone else was in on this, someone up to no good. Hence, the Packard. In my pocket was a roll of blank film. I kept my car keys in my hand in case I had to turn tail and make a run for it.

When I got to the intersection of Mulholland and Pacific View, I saw her seated in the driver's seat of a convertible. The steering wheel was on the right, like an English car. It was the most spectacular car I had ever seen. If this dream were in color, it would be the color of dark, ripe cherries. But these days I only dream in black and white.

Her light blond hair shone in the moonlight. I couldn't decide which was more luminous, her or the car. I decided it was her. I approached, proffering the roll of blank film. I guess it was right then I decided I had to make her mine.

At the same moment, the big black Packard came screeching up from the steep hill where Pacific View took a downward turn toward the Valley. I was momentarily blinded by the headlights. Adeline fired up the V-12.

"Get in," she yelled. I jumped in beside her. "Hold onto your hat!"

It wasn't just a figure of speech. That machine took off like a bat out of hell and my hat nearly went flying.

She took a hard right and we headed west on Mulholland, the Packard in hot pursuit.

"Jeez, what kind of car is this, anyway?" I asked.

"A '39 Delahaye type 165 Cabriolet. It's French; one of six ever made. I took one look and I just had to have it. Hang on…"

We took a sharp left and barreled through a maze of narrow streets winding through the Hollywood Hills. I couldn't see the lights behind us anymore. She suddenly turned off onto a dirt trail and stopped in front of a garage about 200 yards up the road.

"Would you open the garage door, please?" she asked, cool as a cucumber.

I got out, opened the garage, and she pulled the car in. She got out and I closed it up. Next to the garage was a cute little cottage.

"Nobody knows about this place. I come here sometimes when I want to be alone. You're the first person I've ever brought here." She gave me a little smile. I went all gooey inside. But there was light inside the house.

"Why is there a light on?" she said. "There must be somebody in there."

"Maybe we should get out of here."

"No. I've got to see who's in my house."

She took out her keys, but I just turned the knob and the door swung open.

"Hiya, Adie!" It was Albert, a sleazily cheerful young man with slicked-back blond hair (played by Dan Duryea). He was stretched out on her couch.

"What are you doing here, Albert?" Adeline was clearly not pleased to see him.

"Now, is that any way to talk to your dear ol' big brother?"

"How the hell did you know about this place?"

"I'm a very resourceful person, Adie. You should give me more credit."

"What do you want?"

"Aren't you gonna introduce me to your friend?"

"Albert, this is Larry Holden. Mr. Holden, this is Albert Keys, my half-brother. He was banished from the family after he embezzled $25,000 from Father's bank."

"A fine way to introduce me to a stranger. Listen, bud, there's a lot more to the story than that."

"Nobody cares, Albert. You got away with it; let's leave it at that. Now, get out!"

"Not just yet, Adie. I have it on very good account that you are in possession of a roll of film that people are willing to pay a great deal of money for. Even kill for."

"How could you know that?"

"Never mind that." Albert drew a .38 snub nose revolver from his belt. "Just give me the film."

"Why you ungrateful bastard!" cried Adeline. "After I gave you a roof over your head!" I looked at Adeline. "Give it to him," she said.

I tossed Albert the blank roll; he put it in his pocket. "A pleasure doin' business with ya." And off he went.

"You better be packed and gone by the time I get home," she shouted after him.

We heard his car start up and pull away. There were tears in her eyes. I wanted to take her in my arms and hold her so bad I could taste it. Instead, I just looked deep into those eyes. The tears made them deeper and greener than those emeralds. How I knew this in my black-and-white world, I don't know, but I did.

"Suppose you tell me what's going on," I said, barely maintaining my composure.

"Like a drink?"

"Yeah, I could use one."

She poured us both a few fingers of straight scotch. She downed hers in a single gulp and poured herself another.

"I think he's going to use the necklace to blackmail my father," she said tearfully.

"I don't understand."

"Of course you don't. You're not supposed to. It's a secret, see?"

"Before you tell me your secret, I think I'd better tell you mine: that roll of film I gave Albert was blank. The real one is stashed in the trunk of my car—up on Mulholland." I gestured in the general direction of where I thought Mulholland might be, but after all those twists and turns, who could tell? Her face brightened and she gave me a smile that positively gave me goosebumps.

"Why, you darling! You absolute, brilliant darling!" And she kissed me.

It was a kiss that started soft—a gratitude kiss—but then increased in intensity. We kissed long and passionately. I hoped she was feeling what I was feeling because my heart was being taken by storm.

"Now, how can I ever repay you?" she asked with an impish grin. She took me by the hand. "Let me show you the bedroom."

The bedroom was beautifully decked out in bamboo and Japanese paper lanterns. The bed had a polished bamboo headboard that twisted like a pretzel. The bedspread and pillows were also adorned with Japanese motifs: cherry blossoms and lotus leaves. I started to grab her.

"Wait!" she said, holding up her hand. "Just stand right there." She backed up a few paces until she was standing right by the bed. Then she ever so slowly peeled off that silver satin gown. It dropped to the floor around her ankles. She had nothing on underneath. As a young art student in the '30s I had been to Paris, had seen all the great works in the Louvre, but she was the most beautiful thing I had ever laid eyes on. Then she started to fade. Oh no! *Not now. Please, not now!* I became conscious of my shoulder hurting. *Damn!* As I regained consciousness, the dream began to fade from my memory, like always. This time I wasn't going to let it go. I grabbed a pencil and a pad of paper. But by the time I was ready to write it down, all I could remember was Lana Turner standing before me, naked. I tried like hell to hang onto that image, but soon it was only words on paper.

II

I had read some stuff about hypnotherapy. I got the idea that, if a hypno-shrink put me under, perhaps they could get me to remember the dream. I looked for one near me on Yelp. Most were women, and many of them were pretty damn hot-looking. But since I knew there would be sexual content in my dream, I was a bit self-conscious about going to a woman. Besides, most of the therapists listed were not even real doctors — they had credentials after their names like CHT. What was that? I looked a little further afield and found a guy in Beverly Hills by the name of Bryan Schrock, MD. Besides having the MD after his name, instead of the usual lose weight and stop smoking they all touted, his services included *life regression hypnosis*. Being an old hippie, I knew what that meant: he took you back into past lives. I was impressed that any MD would even believe in past lives, let alone take you back into them. No one specifically advertised that they could cure amnesia or help you remember forgotten dreams, so I called Dr. Schrock's office and made an appointment. Luckily, I was able to get in the next day.

The next morning I awoke with a vague recollection of being beaten up by two thugs. I arrived at Dr. Schrock's office on time and was ushered into his inner sanctum about ten minutes later. I had brought my little Zoom digital recorder, an artifact left over from the last of my songwriting days. I wanted to record what I said when I was under and listen to it later.

Schrock was a tall man in his mid-forties, handsome, with receding brown hair combed straight back, and a commanding presence. We shook hands and introduced ourselves.

"Do you do 'Schrock therapy'?" I quipped, in an effort to lighten the mood.

He looked at me and gave me a condescending half smile.

"You've heard that one before."

"Only about a hundred times. But I compliment you on your intelligence. You know what Alfred Hitchcock said?"

"No, what?"

"'Puns are the highest form of literature.'"

Alfred Hitchcock! I knew this was the guy for me.

"Well, that gives me the perfect segue into why I've come to you."

He said nothing, just gave me a look that said *I'm listening*.

I told him about the dream, how it was all one movie, in black and white, 1940s film noir, how every night I got a new installment of the same ongoing story, and how I could never remember the dream upon waking. Just slivers, fragments.

"If you hypnotize me, do you think you can get me to remember the dreams—the dream?"

"It's possible. You say you dream a continuation of the same story every night?"

"Yes. I want you to take me back to the beginning of the story, and I want to record it into this." I showed him the Zoom.

"What do you do during the day?"

"I wait for night."

He laid me out on an extremely comfortable leather recliner. I started recording.

"I'm going to tell every muscle in your body to relax." And then he went through the laundry list, starting with my feet and working his way up.

"Relax your feet, relax your ankles, your calves, your thighs," and so on. "Now, drop your shoulders and relax your arms. Your arms are very, very heavy. Too heavy for you to lift." When he got to my head, he did the back of my neck, my forehead, my temples, and then my eyes. "Your eyelids are very heavy, too heavy for you to open them. Keep them closed. You are more deeply relaxed than you have ever been. Picture a blue sky with ten white clouds. Each cloud has a number on it. Now picture each cloud blowing away. As you blow away each cloud, say its number. As you blow away each cloud you become more and more tired." I started with one and got up to five. Then I was too tired to count clouds anymore. I was way under. The next thing I knew, I was awake and feeling fine.

"Did I remember the dream?"

"You did."

"Why can't I remember anything about this session?"

"Because I told you not to. For some reason you never remember anything about the dream in waking life, and vice versa. I didn't want to tamper with your natural predilections. It's all on there." He indicated the Zoom recorder.

"When can I come back and record more?"

"Come again same time next Wednesday, and we'll record a week's worth of your dream."

It seemed a long time to wait, but I agreed. What follows is what was on the recording I took home:

Dr. Schrock: When did you first have the dream?

Me: Wednesday, May eleventh.

Dr. Schrock: A month ago today.

Me: Yes.

Dr. Schrock: Now you're going back to the beginning, to the first night you had it. Tell me the dream.

The next voice that came out of the recorder was not my own. It was Larry Holden's, a younger, deeper voice than mine. He sounded very authentic, like one of those actors who play the private eye in the '40s movies.

"I'm in my shabby Hollywood apartment. I've converted a laundry room into a darkroom. Prints hang from clips on lines strung up between two walls. It's a tiny room, so I need three lines to accommodate enough prints for a roll of film.

"I get a call from Fritzy Johnson, the editor of the *L.A. Star*. That's a crummy tabloid I work for sometimes. He wants me to go to an address in Hancock Park that night, the Wadsworth Mansion, to photograph everyone who emerges from the fancy cars and limos as they pull up for the Governor's Ball. 'It starts at nine. Get there early,' he says…"

As I listened, I could visualize everything perfectly.

The rest, although all of this was completely new to me in my waking life, I have already recounted — right up to Lana Turner playing Adeline standing before me naked, so I'll just skip ahead to that scene…

*

Adeline reached out and took my hand, gently pulling me down onto the bed. She started unbuttoning my shirt, then undid my belt. I shed the rest of my clothes in record time. She was the wildest, least-inhibited girl I had ever known. (Thank God there was no Hollywood production code to censor my dream movie.) We did things that night I had only read about in dirty magazines, things they only have words for in France. It was, in short, the fuck of my life. If I was hooked before, now I was completely landed, flopping around on the pier, helpless and gasping for breath. I was hers, hook, line, and sinker.

Afterward, we laid around, smoking.

"Where did you learn tricks like that?"

"Nowhere," she said emphatically. I gave her a skeptical

look. "No, really. I just did what came naturally. Okay, I'm not a virgin. I did it once before—and it was terrible: five seconds of feverish pumping then, 'night-night.' But I swear, Larry, I've never experienced anything like this before ... I think I might love you."

"So what are we gonna do about it?"

"Nothing. This is terribly inconvenient."

"That's one word for it."

"I could never marry anyone poor."

"Of course not. And who could blame you? I couldn't support even a regular girl, let alone someone like you."

"So don't propose, okay?"

"Don't worry."

"'Cause I might say yes. And then we'd both be in a lot of trouble."

I turned her to face me. "We already are, baby."

We kissed. If either of us thought this wasn't the real thing, we were kidding ourselves. Still, I had lingering doubts about her story of *doing what came naturally*. This girl had experience, but, at that point, I didn't care.

There was a long silence. "Well," I said, "What d'ya say we get up to Mulholland and get the real film before my car gets towed ... and make me $5,000 closer to being rich."

We put our clothes on, then she locked up the house.

The sun was just coming up as we drove back through the winding deserted streets.

"So now you tell me: What is it about this necklace that makes everybody want to get that film? How could your brother use it to blackmail your father?"

"I—I don't know."

I gave her a look that said *Aw, c'mon.*

"No, really. I just know there's some secret surrounding that necklace and my father doesn't want it to get out. I should never have put it on. He forbade me to ever wear it, or even speak of it. It's not supposed to exist. That's all I know."

"Well, a whole lot of other people sure seem to know it exists. Who was following us in that Packard?"

"I have no idea. I think that's your car up there…"

She made a U-turn and pulled up behind my car. I got out and opened the trunk.

"What made you take a blank roll and hide the real film in your trunk?"

"When you called me, there was a second click after you hung up. Someone was listening in, so I knew there was gonna be trouble."

"Probably Albert," she said.

I leaned into the trunk to fish out the film and suddenly the Packard appeared out of nowhere and screeched to a halt beside us. Two men got out and pulled guns. One was big and looked like an over-the-hill boxer who had taken one too many shots to the head. The other was the guy I had seen at the Wadsworth Mansion, the one who was clocking me. He was smaller, with cruel eyes and a crooked smile. This one had enough brains to be really dangerous. I could see there was someone in the back seat of the Packard, a man in a hat, but I couldn't get a good look at him.

"Hand over the film, smart guy," said the small mean one.

The back door of the car opened and out stepped the man in the hat. He was a short, stocky guy with thick lips. He chewed on a big cigar and wore an expensive topcoat. He had the look of the streets, but the edges were smoothed out a bit. In my dream, he was played by Edward G. Robinson. (Of course. I must've seen *Double Indemnity* fifteen times). "Take it easy, Rollo. I'm sure Mr. Holden will cooperate." He reached into his pocket and flashed some kind of badge. It wasn't an LAPD badge. "Vincent Schiaparelli, Allied Insurance Company."

"Insurance? What d'ya want with me?" I asked.

"The necklace."

"What necklace?" Adeline and I asked as one.

"Don't bullshit me. Excuse the French, miss, but Rollo here saw you wearing it." He turned to me. "And he saw you take the picture." Adeline and I continued to play dumb. "They're known as the Burdell emeralds."

Burdell was Adeline's mother's maiden name.

"Let me refresh your memories. You were both kids at the time, but in 1929, this necklace was supposedly stolen from the Keys mansion. Your father was wiped out in the crash, so he had a good motive to commit insurance fraud, and I think that's exactly what he did. He had city hall in his pocket at the time, so the cops handled the investigation with kid gloves. Intentionally sloppy. The United Insurance Company ended up paying out a million dollars to your pop after no one could come up with any clues whatsoever. This and the depression caused United to go bankrupt. Keys thought he was home free, but my company, Allied, bought United out of bankruptcy, and I've decided to reopen the case. We're offering a $100,000 reward to whoever turns in the emeralds. Of course, we'd have to prosecute your father —unless he paid back the million United gave him. With interest, of course."

Adeline and I just looked at each other and kept silent.

"The film, Mack," said Rollo.

I reached into the trunk and got the roll of film. I handed it to Rollo but kept hold of the tag of film I always leave sticking out so I can easily extract it for development. When he grabbed the canister, I pulled on the end of the film and the whole roll came spilling out all over Mulholland Drive, exposing and ruining all the negatives.

"Why, you..."

The little guy slugged me behind my left ear with the butt of his gun. I saw stars. Reflexively, I took a swing at him. He caught it in his left eye and went down. I immediately felt that familiar queasiness in my stomach. It happens every time I hit somebody.

I was born in New York City. Hell's Kitchen. Both my parents died in the flu epidemic of 1918. I was three. They put me and my two brothers in an orphanage. It was—harsh, to say the least. Both my brothers died there. I ran away when I was ten. I had to fight a lot to survive on the streets of New York. But ever since I fought my best friend on a rooftop over something stupid and I slugged him and he fell off and died, violence has made me physically ill.

Then the big guy stepped in and started pounding away on my face. I was too sick to fight back. The last thing I heard before everything went black was Adeline screaming, "Leave him alone!"

The pain went from my head to my left shoulder, and I woke up, lying on my left side in my dreary, full-color bedroom.

III

Life dragged on at its petty pace until Wednesday rolled around. I felt like a kid at Christmas as I took my little recorder and headed over to Dr. Schrock's office. Here's what was on the Zoom when I got it home.

*

I came to in the driver's seat of my car. My hat was pulled down over my eyes. Something hard was poking me in the shoulder. I lifted the brim to see a cop poking me with his nightstick. There was a patrol car with another cop in it parked behind me.

"Wake up, buddy. You can't sleep here ... say, what happened to you?"

My head seemed to be enlarging and shrinking in rhythmic waves of pain, accompanied by a humming sound that got louder when my head expanded and softer when it contracted.

How long had I been out? No way to tell. The Packard was gone, and so was Adeline's car. I had to come up with a credible story fast, and my brain was really in no condition.

"Well, let me see..."

"Hey, what's this?" asked cop number two, picking up the mangled roll of film from the pavement behind my car.

"I'm a photographer," I said. It seemed like a good idea to start off with something true. "I sell a lot of shots to the *Star*." Then a story just magically materialized. It's amazing what the brain is capable of when one's ass is on the line. "I crashed a party last night around here somewhere, and there were some celebrities and movie stars there, and I snapped some pictures. They didn't like it and had a couple of bouncers throw me out and work me over."

"Where's your camera?" asked cop number one.

"I don't know. They probably took it or smashed it up. That film is what I shot last night. I guess they exposed the whole roll."

"Let's see some ID," said cop number one. I reached into my inside pocket for my wallet and felt an envelope that wasn't there before. I showed him my press card from the *Star*.

"Okay, get outta here" — he looked at the card — "'Larry.' And stop pokin' your nose where it don't belong."

I could barely see straight, but I had to find Adeline. I decided to drive over to the Keys mansion. On the way, I pulled the envelope out of my pocket. In it were fifty hundred-dollar bills. On the envelope, she had scribbled an address on Broad Beach Road, way out in Malibu. Then I noticed a crumpled up brown paper bag on the floor of my car. I pulled over and picked it up. In it were the Burdell emeralds.

I headed for Malibu.

※

The address Adeline had written was for a large bungalow perched about thirty feet above the beach. It was way above

Malibu, at Trancas, and this was the only house within 200 yards. I didn't see Adeline's car. I took the brown paper bag and locked it in my trunk, then rang the doorbell. No answer. I waited a few minutes, then rang again.

I faintly heard a woman's voice from deep inside the house. "I'm comin', I'm comin'. Hold yer horses!" Then the shuffling of old-woman feet.

After another minute, the door was opened by an elderly housekeeper. "Well?" she asked irritably.

"My name is Holden. Is Adeline Keys here?"

Without responding, she turned and walked through the foyer. "This way." She led me into a comfortably appointed living room. "Wait in here," she said. "Don't bother trying to get a drink. She keeps the liquor locked up."

"You'll have to excuse Hattie. She's not known for her social graces." It was an elderly, aristocratic lady (played by Ethel Barrymore) with kind, sharp eyes, standing in the doorway. She scrutinized me carefully. "Are you Mr. Holden?"

"Yes, ma'am."

She turned to the housekeeper. "That'll be all, Hattie. You can go to bed." Hattie shuffled upstairs. "Sit down, won't you? Adeline said to expect you. I'm Clara Leighton, Adeline's aunt—her father's sister. Adeline should be here in a while. I got a call from her earlier. She used her father's private line. We don't think it's tapped. She's bringing her father. They're going into hiding."

"Here?"

"No. This is just the first stop."

I took off my hat and stepped into the light.

"My God, what did they do to you? Lie down on the couch. I'll get some ice." I did as I was told. She went off to the kitchen and came back with a makeshift ice pack, made with a hot water bottle and some ice cubes. "Here, put this on that lump behind your ear." Then she got a washcloth and cleaned my face up a bit. I'd been on my own since I was ten, and it felt good to be mothered. She gave me some aspirin and water. Then offered me a tall scotch, which I accepted eagerly.

"Those guys that worked me over. They're insurance investigators."

"Yes, Adeline told me."

"I'm pretty certain they'll follow her."

"She knows that. She was expecting them to knock on the door at any moment when she called. She expects they'll want to search the house. While they're busy searching, her plan is to spirit her father out through a secret passageway that leads from his inner sanctum to the garage, and get a head start on them."

"Her brother, Albert. He's got it in for Adeline and your brother. I think he's in with the thugs. There's a big reward for that necklace."

"Yes. I know the whole story. Albert's always been a bad kid. Oh my god! I just realized — Adeline and Albert used to come out here when they were children in the summertime. Albert knows about this place!"

"Then he'll probably lead the insurance thugs right to us."

"Adeline told me she gave you the necklace. Do you have it?"

I hesitated, but I trusted her, so answered honestly. "Yeah."

"Where is it?"

"In the trunk of my car."

"Can you get it?"

I went outside and opened the trunk. Then I heard footsteps.

"Hiya, Larry ol' pal." It was Albert. I turned to see him with his .38 pointed right at me. "Don't tell me she gave *you* the bauble. This is even better than I planned!" He came closer. "You don't pack iron, do ya?"

"No." I opened my coat and showed him.

"Then just hand it over, pal."

As he reached for the bag, I accidentally-on-purpose let the necklace fall to the ground. In that split second, as he watched it drop, I caught him with a hard right on the chin. He dropped like a stone. I grabbed the gun.

And that's where the recording ended.

IV

The next day I resolved to do something that involved other people.

Since I had retired two years ago, I'd lived on a very modest fixed income in the rent-controlled apartment I had occupied for twenty years. There was little room in my budget for social activities. I almost never saw anyone. I spoke on the phone with a few old friends, but they all lived very far away. I wouldn't say I was lonely exactly, but I did feel a certain sense of isolation.

My last relationship with a woman had ended six years ago when I was still working and earning what most would consider a middle-class income. But not Margot. Margot had been married to a cartoonist who stumbled into the video game business in its infancy, in the early '80s. He'd designed a war game that made him millions. When they divorced, Margot walked away with three million dollars. In addition, she was an executive at a travel firm and pulled down a salary of $80,000 a year. But, for some reason, she loved me. Or said she loved me. She was beautiful and sexy and had a great house, so what could be bad? I fell for her like an avalanche. Then, after almost exactly a year of unwedded bliss, she sent me an email. We used to trade funny little rhymes. I had started it. I liked making them up for people's birthday cards, and this bled over to my relationship with Margot. But this email wasn't funny. It was entitled "A Sad Poem." What it lacked in literary merit, it made up for in emotional impact; it knocked my guts out.

> *I'm sorry to say this, my dear, but it is true,*
> *I love you so, but I am blue.*
> *I need more in life, that only money can buy*
> *This is how we are different, oh why, oh why?*
> *I can't carry us both, financially speaking,*
> *This entire poem is leaving me weeping.*

There was more, not in verse: she said she was miserable and admitted to being a chicken. I had never asked her to carry me financially, but I had made the fatal error of accepting a couple of loans from her. They were her idea, but I never should have gone along. When I was finally able to get through to her on the phone, she explained that she was never unhappy with me, but she needed to find someone with *financial parity* to her. It didn't have to be someone rich, just equal.

I remained in a state of shock and grief for several years. After that, I made no attempt to get back into the dating game. And, every time I looked in the mirror, the old man I saw there confirmed I had made the right decision.

But today I decided to attend a meeting of a neighborhood association whose main mission was to restrict the unbridled development taking place in my beloved town of Santa Monica. I had been getting emailed announcements for these meetings for maybe a year. I always marked them on my calendar, intending to go, but never went. I decided I would go tonight. The Montana Branch of the Santa Monica Public Library, where the meeting was being held, was a walk of maybe five blocks.

I got there before the meeting actually began, during the pre-meeting schmooze. Most of the attendees were elderly, like me. People in their fifties and older. These were my fellow long-time Santa Monica residents who didn't want the neighborhood to change, didn't want the rental laws protecting them to change, and didn't want to be forced out of their homes at this stage in life. I didn't know anyone there, but I did notice one attractive woman. She could have been in her fifties, although she looked much younger. The only thing that betrayed her age was her graying hair, which, had she chosen to dye it, would have made me conclude she was way too young for me. I admired that she didn't dye it. A lot of people in my neighborhood are physical fitness fanatics, organic eaters, yoga practitioners, especially the women. I pegged her for one of these.

To my surprise, she turned to me, looked me straight in the eye, and smiled. It was a lovely smile, and clearly an invitation.

"Hi," she said.

I introduced myself.

"Sharon Johnson," she said, "you live around here?"

"Yeah. 16th and California. You?"

"Idaho and 17th."

"So we live three blocks from each other."

"And I don't even know the people who live next door," she said.

"Must be serendipity," I said.

She had beautiful blue eyes. My last girlfriend had blue eyes, but she lived in Ventura County. Very inconvenient. But we'd managed to get together two or three nights a week, taking turns driving to each other's houses. After that, I resolved that I would only consider a serious romance with someone within walking—or at least biking—distance. Sharon rose to the standard admirably.

We sat next to each other at the meeting. I mostly listened. The speaker was a woman on the City Council, someone whom we had elected on her professed platform of opposition to the big development projects and changes in zoning laws now being considered by the Santa Monica City government.

At the Q&A Sharon raised her hand.

"What I want to know is this: Why did I, and all the others here, who voted for you, vote for you? You ran on an 'anti-development' platform, and then you stabbed us in the back and voted to approve that giant mixed-use structure at Arizona and 5th Street. What's up with that?"

"That development will contain public park land and affordable housing," said the councilwoman.

"That is a half-truth," said Sharon. "The 'public park land' you speak of would be mostly on the roof and patios of a gargantuan office building, and there would only be four or five affordable apartment units—out of fifty. Mainly, it would contain offices to which nine thousand commuters would drive and park their nine thousand cars every day."

Sharon was smart and well-informed. She impressed me enormously.

"Can I walk you home?" I asked after the meeting.

"Sure."

We talked about our interests—some of them mutual. We were both into classic rock and a few old new-wave groups. It turned out she was the widow of the lead guitarist of a famous British band who had died of a drug overdose back in 1981. The band, which will remain nameless here, was one of my all-time favorites. She was also heavy into yoga and Buddhist philosophy, something else we shared. I told her a little about my career as an almost-rock-star—I had been leader and songwriter for several bands in the '60s, '70s, and '80s, some of which were signed to major record companies —then as an A&R guy for a couple of record companies. In the early 2000s the record business imploded and I developed my skills as a writer, editor, and proofreader. I had a brief career as a copywriter for several ad agencies before I'd decided to retire.

"So, way too much about me. What's your story?"

"I'm a film editor. Mostly documentaries and a few minor features so far. But I feel fortunate to be making a living at the thing I love."

We were both fans of the black-and-white movies of old. When we got to her building, we exchanged phone numbers and emails and agreed to keep in touch.

Walking home, I mused about the possibilities. I knew I liked her and was attracted to her and I suspected she felt the same. This could represent a major life change for me. I had been a virtual recluse for several years. Another thing making it ideal was that we each had our own apartment, close enough to see each other at any time, but also a place to which we could each escape if we needed to. After three marriages and a few brief cohabitations, I knew beyond any doubt that I could never actually live with anyone ever again. For me, Sharon had all the makings of a perfect companion.

I waited a day or two, then called and asked her out to dinner. We went to Thai Dishes, the best Thai restaurant in all of LA and it was within walking distance of both our places. Sitting across from her at the table I was able to gaze into those clear blue eyes and I liked the way she was looking at me.

After dinner, we walked home. The June moon was bright and nearly full.

"Hey, you wanna see my place?" I said. "It's right on the way to yours."

I have good apartment karma. I got into this place twenty-two years ago, just before rent control became a thing of the past. It's on the ground floor, at the rear of a two-unit building. It's just a one bedroom, but it's nice. There's plenty of space for me and my cat, who comes in and out as he pleases. Outside, there's a patio with a table and chairs and a metal roof supported by filigreed wrought iron posts. Then there's a little lawn. My yard is sheltered from the property next door by a row of Cyprus trees that form a solid wall of green. There are potted plants all around. It's very quiet and private, sort of like a little guest house.

"My god, this is so charming," she said.

"It's perfect for me. C'mon in."

I put on a CD by a little-known female artist I really like called Joy Askew.

I was happy to learn Sharon was a fellow drinker. I made myself a brandy and soda and she had white wine.

"Put on that vanity album you told me about," she said.

I was somewhat reticent to follow Joy, whose singing and songwriting is magnificent, but I played her the album I had made at my own expense several years ago. I hadn't promoted it, except to my friends on Facebook, and it sold about four copies. I didn't like my singing on it, but the songs were solid, if not current-sounding.

"I love it," said Sharon. "Especially that song 'Overboard.'"

I could see she wasn't bullshitting me. We ended up kissing and making out—something I hadn't done for six years.

At last, she sighed. "I really have to go. I have to get up early in the morning."

I was glad it hadn't gone any further. Over long years of experience in these matters, I've learned that rushing into bed with someone you hardly know is never a good idea. I walked her the three blocks to her place. I got a brief tour of her apartment, which had two floors and was much larger than mine. I was really impressed with her taste in décor. She had some embroidered Tibetan thangkas that must have cost a fortune, as well as a Buddha on an altar of sorts with incense, and some impressive Western art as well.

We kissed goodnight and I walked home under the bright moon, enervated and dazed.

✻

That night I slept soundly and dreamed I was part of a hippie tribe in Northern California. The dream was in full color and I remembered a lot of it. It was the first time in months I hadn't dreamed a continuation of the film noir story of Larry and Adeline. I was alarmed and dismayed. I had grown very attached to my black-and-white adventure, and I wanted to know how it came out in the end. I wondered if it was gone forever. I wondered if it had anything to do with my growing feelings for Sharon.

Monday morning, I put in a call to Dr. Schrock, left a message with his assistant asking him to call me. A few hours later he called back. I told him what had happened and about Sharon. I wondered if he could hypnotize me into going back to the black-and-white dream. He said he didn't know. I decided to keep my regular Wednesday appointment.

Meanwhile, I kept thinking about Sharon. I wanted to see her again. I didn't want her to think I wasn't interested. I saw that the Aero, our local Santa Monica art cinema, was showing a revival of two Fellini films: *La Dolce Vita* and *8½*. I had seen both of them multiple times, but not in a theater in a long time. I called Sharon and asked if she wanted to go, maybe one night during the week, as I hated to go to movies on weekend nights. She said Wednesday would be good.

The rest of the week, I dreamed every night—in color—of insignificant things. It became clear I'd reverted to the standard dreaming I had always done before the advent of Adeline and Larry.

I saw Dr. Schrock Wednesday afternoon. He put me under and suggested I resume the dream of Adeline and Larry. He said that was all he could think of to do, and if I truly wanted to go back to that dream, I probably would. He agreed with me that the arrival of Sharon had probably triggered the change. He encouraged me to live my life while I was awake. "You'll be a long time dead," he concluded cheerfully.

"When we're dead, do you think we go to the place of our dreams?"

He shrugged. "That's as good a theory as any."

※

That evening, I met Sharon at a popular eatery on Montana, not far from the Aero. We had a bite to eat and Sharon told me about her wild life as the wife of a rock star in England. This was at the beginning of the punk revolution, which happened almost exactly a decade after the Beatles revolution, the time of my first foray into rock 'n' roll. Sharon's husband's band was neither pure punk nor pure new wave, but rather a hybrid that bridged both worlds, which made them unique and, I dare say, immortal. After her husband's death, Sharon moved to New York City (my home town), where she studied film at NYU. She married a prominent architect and had a daughter, who became a successful model. I was shocked to learn she was fifty-eight years old. She looked much younger, but this fact gave me hope. Even though I was a decade older, there was a chance for a relationship.

After dinner, we walked to the theater. It was good seeing those old Fellini films again on the big screen. I especially loved *La Dolce Vita*, which was in black and white. Walking back toward my place, we discussed the films. She was a really astute viewer, being a professional editor. I remarked that, in all the fiction-writing classes I had taken—both as a college undergraduate and later as an adult—they had always stressed the importance of a story arc: a beginning, a middle, and an end, raising and dropping the tension until it built to a crescendo, a denouement of some kind, a resolution. I remarked that *La Dolce Vita* had none of that. It was just a series of scenes from a guy's life in which he gets increasingly decadent and emotionally lost. And it worked beautifully.

"You know, I've been flailing about looking for a story idea and I think I might have just gotten one."

"Tell me," she said.

"Well, when I was thirteen I had this friend from 'the other side of the tracks.' His name was Richie and he was a true juvenile delinquent. He was always dreaming up crazy stunts. Dangerous and destructive stunts. And I became his partner in crime. His enabler, you might say. No one actually got hurt or killed, but the potential was always there."

"Sounds intriguing," she said.

"But, here's the thing: I could write this like *La Dolce Vita*; just a series of scenes in the life of these two boys. No story arc."

"I say go for it," she said.

"Thank you, muse," I said, only half-joking.

When we got to my house, I invited her in. We had drinks, we made out, and we wound up in bed together. Her body was, as Michael Caine said in *Alfie*, in beautiful condition. She looked a lot better than I did, that's for sure. I was nervous. I hadn't done this in six years, and I wasn't sure I still could. Maybe I was too old; maybe I had lost it. But she was incredibly open and affectionate and put me at my ease, and everything worked out pretty well for a first time.

*

Dr. Schrock's hypnotic suggestion didn't work. That night I dreamed I had a job driving an eighteen-wheel trailer truck. The cab was a bright blue, making it look more like a toy than a real truck. I knew I was doing a lousy job. I felt really bad about myself. My boss was very kind and understanding, but he just shook his head sadly. He knew I was hopeless as a truck driver and he very gently fired me. It was just like a job I once had as a proofreader. The copy was of a highly technical nature, and there was an array of different legal language that had to be adhered to exactly for each of various different subsidiaries. I knew I was out of my depth, but I hung on as long as I could because the money was really good. After a few gentle warnings that I wasn't cutting it, my boss sadly told me this would be my last day. My coworkers were very nice about it. "This isn't for everyone," they said. But the feeling of failure haunted me for quite a while—until I got a new job as a copywriter. Much less challenging and much more fun.

It looked like my black-and-white world of Adeline and Larry was gone forever. In spite of my happiness at finding Sharon, there was a pervasive sadness in my heart that surfaced every time I thought about Adeline. And I wondered what would become of her in that parallel universe.

※

Sharon and I continued to see each other and have sex a couple of times a week. She had just started work on a major Hollywood picture. It was a plum job and she was anxious to make good. She worked long hours and on weekends, and I didn't get to see her as often. Although I called her almost every night, it was rare that I actually got to speak with her, and before long, weeks had passed and we hadn't spoken. Finally, she called me back.

"I'm so sorry. It's been a strange time for me." Her voice was filled with trepidation.

"What's wrong, Sharon?"

"I-I hardly know how to begin. I've been seeing someone else."

"Ouch," I said.

"Yeah, ouch."

"Anybody I know?"

"It's Jason Corelli, the director on the picture I've been editing."

Jason Corelli was a big name in Hollywood. He was younger than both me and her, and vastly richer and more powerful.

"I understand completely. No hard feelings. I wish you nothing but good things," I said, concealing my jealousy of the other man's clear superiority. This was, after all, Hollywood.

I felt an odd mix of emotions: pain and wounded pride at being rebuffed and at the same time a certain relief and a kind of hopefulness that perhaps my black-and-white dream world would now return. I now realized that at some level, I resented Sharon for taking Adeline away from me.

V

I started working on my short story, a semi-autobiographical recounting of an adventure out of my juvenile delinquent past. I decided to call it "J.D.," and true to *La Dolce Vita*, there was no story arc. After a few rewrites, I was pretty pleased with the way it read. I found a long online list of literary magazines that accepted submissions and I began submitting "J.D." to all the ones that looked like they might go for something like this. It was an arduous process, but it kept me busy and kept my mind off the loss of my black-and-white dream world and the rejection I had suffered from Sharon.

Then the rejection letters started arriving. They were mostly form letters that basically said, in the gentlest terms possible, the same thing: that they had read it with interest, but it just wasn't right for their publication. All but one, which actually gave me personalized feedback: no story arc. In all, 149 publications rejected my piece. Then, one rainy day, I found in my mailbox an envelope that I recognized as one of my self-addressed, stamped envelopes, which had accompanied one of the few hard copy submissions I had made. *Another rejection*, I thought. But when I opened the soggy envelope, in it was a small slip of paper about two inches by three inches. On it was a letterhead from a magazine called *Manifesto*. There was a note sloppily scribbled in blue ink. Here is what it said:

> Dear Mr. — and then my last name,
> OK (then something crossed out) On "J.D."
> (These "slice of life" stories are killing me).
> You'll receive two copies and a penny a word
> for the first North American serial rights.
> Thank you.
> Happy New Year!
> Jonathan Blum

This seemed to be an acceptance letter. I had never received one, so I wasn't sure. I showed it to a friend, and she confirmed: it *was* an acceptance letter! I immediately retraced my submission steps and went to the website of *Manifesto*. All it said was "Website Expired." All I had was a street address for Mr. Blum, so I wrote him a short note that had a photocopy of his acceptance letter at the bottom. I thanked him for accepting my story. Told him I couldn't wait to see it in print. Then I mentioned I had tried to go to his website and found it expired. I asked if he could please shoot me a quick email to the address on my letterhead and let me know what was going on. Had *Manifesto* gone belly-up? (Those were not my exact words.) I went back to the master list of literary magazines I had used as a resource and *Manifesto* was no longer listed.

I never received a reply.

*

Every night, I would knock myself out in the customary manner and hope that my black-and-white dream would return. But no such luck. I decided to give Dr. Schrock another try. I called and made an appointment for the following Wednesday.

Dr. Schrock put me under again and suggested I continue my black-and-white dream but to no avail.

※

The days and nights dragged on. I thought about trying to write my dream as a story, but it would just come out sounding like a cliché film noir plot—like one of those movies they made by the dozen in the '40s, or—if I was lucky—like a Raymond Chandler novel.

I went to another community meeting at the library. I didn't contribute; just listened. I wasn't that well informed about local politics, but I knew it was on the local level one could really make an impact on one's daily existence. I spotted Sharon seated a few rows in front of me. She didn't see me.

After the meeting, I just got up and walked out. I didn't feel like mingling. Then I heard her footsteps coming up fast behind me. She caught up with me and said "Hi."

"Hi," I said. "How're things going?"

"Oh, busy." Her voice had a forlorn quality.

"How's the new relationship working out?"

"It didn't. The guy's an asshole. Big surprise. A major Hollywood director. What did I expect?"

"Sorry," I said.

"I made a big mistake to leave you. You're a great guy. You didn't deserve that ... I don't suppose you'd be interested in us seeing each other again?"

This came as a complete surprise to me. In fact, I don't think anyone had ever come crawling back to me. I thought about it for a long moment. I hadn't really missed Sharon all that much—not as much as I missed Adeline. And it was because of Sharon that I lost Adeline. "I don't think it would work, Sharon. I wouldn't want to leave myself open for another blindside and I don't think I could ever really trust you again."

Her eyes teared up. She looked really pretty that way. "Okay, sure. I understand. You take care." And she walked off fast.

I'm a little ashamed to admit it, but it gave me a rush to turn her down; to see her walk away with tears in her eyes. It made me feel powerful, attractive. Things I hadn't felt about myself in a very long time.

And, that night, Adeline came back to me.

VI

As soon as I fell asleep, the dream picked up right where it had left off. When I awoke, I knew it had returned, and immediately called Dr. Schrock and made an appointment. When I played back the recording, I heard me speaking in Larry's voice...

※

I shoved the necklace back in the crumpled paper bag and took it inside, leaving Albert temporarily sprawled in the driveway. I put the bag on the table in front of Mrs. Leighton.

"What are you planning to do with this?" I asked.

"When Adeline gets here, we're going to deep-six it."

"Deep-six?"

"Literally. You and she are going to take the motorboat that's tied to the end of the dock behind my house, sail out a ways, and toss this geegaw into the briny deep."

I excused myself, went to the bathroom, and threw up.

"What's wrong, Larry? You look green."

"I always throw up after I hit someone. It's a long story, Aunt Clara—is it okay if I call you that?"

"Delighted."

"Do you have some rope?"

"Rope?"

"Yeah. Enough to tie a guy up."

"I think so. Why?"

"Because your nephew Albert is passed out in your driveway and I have to tie him up." I showed her the gun. "He pulled this on me and tried to take the necklace, so I had to knock him out."

"Well, bravo! A few feet of rope, coming up. Will you need any help getting him into the house?"

"Nope. I think I can manage." She got the rope. I went back outside and bound Albert's legs together at the ankles. I grabbed an arm and managed to sling him over my shoulder, fireman-style. I carried him into the house and we sat him in a wooden chair. I tied his hands behind his back and him to the chair.

"Larry," said Aunt Clara. "Do you want to tell me why you were sick?"

"Let's just say it's something that happens to me every time I slug a guy and leave it at that. Looks like Sleeping Beauty is coming to..."

Albert shook his head, noticed he was bound hand and foot. "What the hell...?"

"Uh-uh-uh. Ladies present," I said.

"Ow. I think you busted my jaw, you ... dirty rat!"

"If it were busted, you wouldn't be talking so much."

"We were kind of expecting you, Albert," Aunt Clara chimed in. "I realized—a bit late—that you and Adeline used to visit here when you were kids."

"Oh, hi, Aunt Clara. Nice to see you again," said Albert.

"Did you lead the insurance boys here?" I asked.

"They have the address. I expect they'll be along directly."

"How did they get my address, Albert?" said Aunt Clara.

"I've been workin' for them from the beginning. I was their inside man, you might say. Heck, I knew Adie was gonna wear that necklace before she did."

"How?" I asked.

"Jerome. I was supplying him with opium, getting him drunk on rum. He knew everything about the necklace—even the combination to Dad's secret safe. Heck, he was the one who pulled the job for Dad in the first place. He had a peephole from his room into the old man's. He saw Adie sneak into his room at night and just stare at the thing. I knew she would be tempted to wear it, and I guessed the Governor's Ball would be the time. That's how the insurance dicks knew to be there, watching."

"But Adeline told me you were gonna blackmail your father," I said.

"Nah. It was never blackmail. Schiaparelli hired me to help him with the investigation. He had this feeling in his gut the necklace was still around. So he put me on retainer and offered me the hundred grand reward if they recovered the necklace."

"But what about Adeline? Did she make her getaway?" asked Aunt Clara anxiously. "Are the insurance guys chasing her?"

"She used the secret passageway to get her and the old man out of the house, so she had a big head start on them. In that car of hers, I'm surprised she didn't beat me here," said Albert.

Just then the doorbell rang. From upstairs I heard Hattie grumbling, "Now what? What is this, Grand Central Station?"

"That's all right, Hattie. I'll get it," said Aunt Clara. She opened the door, and there stood Adeline and Mr. Keys, both looking much the worse for wear. Adeline helped her father, who walked with two canes and some difficulty. They were both covered in dark brown topsoil. "My goodness, whatever happened to you?" cried Aunt Clara.

I rushed over and put my arms around her. I was so relieved I kissed her in front of everyone, without regard for decorum.

"Aww, ain't love grand," said Albert. "So, what *did* happen?"

"Albert! You here already? Bet you're sorry to see me — alive!" said Adeline. "We were being tailed by the insurance guys. I was going rather fast. We were barreling down the big hill on Malibu Canyon Road toward Pacific Coast Highway when my brakes went." She gave Albert a significant look. "I'll bet you dimes to dollars *someone* cut the brake line and all the fluid leaked out."

"What're you lookin' at me for?" said Albert.

"Who would have a better reason for wanting both me and Father dead? Why then you'd inherit his entire fortune by default."

"That's a serious accusation, Adie. I hope you're prepared to prove it," said Albert.

"I'll try, Albert. I'll really try. Why are you all tied up?"

Albert looked at me sheepishly. "I had to take his toy away," I said, showing her the gun. "He wanted the necklace."

"Well," said Adeline, "while you're in this compromising position, I have something for you, Albert." And she walked over and slapped him hard in the face.

All the while, Mr. Keys slouched in an easy chair nursing a small flask. "Masterful driving," he said almost to himself, slurring his words. "You should have seen her, weaving in and out of oncoming cars. It was thrilling!" Then he noticed his surroundings and his sister. "I don't believe I've had the pleasure, dear lady," he said to Clara.

"I'm Clara, Monty. Your sister."

"Clara? But you're so old!"

"We're both old, Monty. Finish your story, Adeline. How did you survive?"

"Near the bottom, the hillside is made of soft dirt. I just steered as gently as I could into the hillside, wrecked the right side of my car, got a whole lot of dirt in my lap, but it stopped the car."

"How did you get here?" asked Aunt Clara.

"We hitchhiked," said Adeline.

"Charming couple," muttered Mr. Keys. "I think they were on their honeymoon."

Meanwhile, Albert was glowering at Adeline and the adoring way I was looking at her.

"I wonder what your boyfriend would say if he knew what you really are, Adie."

"What do you mean?" Something about this guy made me really want to hurt him.

"Your girlfriend is nothing but a tramp, Larry my boy—a party girl. She and her pal Reggie throw sex parties—regular orgies. She does it with guys, two at once, girls, farm animals, you name it. Adie gets passed around like the church collection plate on Sunday."

"Why, you lyin'..." I tasted bile rising in my throat, and I was about to haul off on him again, but Adeline's voice stopped me.

"It's true, Larry."

I froze. I took one look at her tear-filled eyes and the shame on her face and knew it was so.

"I've been bad. Very, very bad. But I love you and it will never happen again. Can you forgive me?"

I felt like I had turned to stone. Except for my eyes, which were filling with tears. I kept picturing her with all those guys. This explained why she repaid me by taking me to bed when we hadn't known each other an hour. And I thought it was love at first sight. How could I have been so stupid? I said nothing.

"None of them meant anything to me. I was drunk. We were all drunk—and high on drugs. Reggie dared me, he taunted me, said I didn't have the nerve. Well, I sure showed him." She broke down sobbing.

Aunt Clara was clearly shocked, and red with embarrassment. Even Mr. Keys snapped out of his stupor and stared, slack-jawed, at his beloved daughter.

Just then there was a loud pounding on the door. We all looked at each other.

"It seems they've arrived," said Aunt Clara. Then the front door burst open, with the two thugs in the lead, guns drawn, followed by Vincent Schiaparelli.

"Everybody, hands in the air ... except you," said Rollo, noticing Albert. The insurance guys all snickered.

"Well, hail, hail, the gang's all here," said Schiaparelli.

"You. Drop that cannon," said Rollo, looking at me. I was still in a state of shock and didn't even hear him. I barely noticed the thugs enter the room. "I said drop it, buster!" I dropped the gun and put my hands up.

"Now you drop yours, boys!"

It was Hattie, the old housekeeper. She wielded a twelve-gauge shotgun. Schiaparelli and his henchmen had entered the living room and Hattie had descended the stairs behind them, ever so quietly. She cocked both barrels. "I've got one barrel for each of you two. And make no mistake, when I shoot, I don't miss. Now drop the guns, turn around, and hands up!"

I quickly retrieved all the guns, gave one to Aunt Clara, and put the other two in my pockets.

"Now, take the bag, Adeline, and you two make a run for it," said Aunt Clara. Adeline picked up the paper bag and headed out the back door that led to a rickety wooden staircase and down to the dock. I was still in shock. I followed her down there, slowly.

She looked back at me. "Are you coming?"

I just shook my head. I couldn't get the visions of her doing those things with other guys out of my head.

A mist had started to roll in over the Pacific. She jumped into the launch and cast off the bow line, then stood in the stern looking back at me. She took the necklace from the paper bag and put it on, yanked on the cord, and started the engine. She was still wearing the silver satin gown, all muddied, with a black coat draped over her shoulders and a black beret. The necklace completed the picture perfectly. The little boat chugged out to sea. She raised her hand in a static salute of goodbye. I waved back as if in a trance and watched her recede, a frozen tableau, a bejeweled Joan of Arc, into the fog.

I didn't know what she had in mind. Would she go down with the necklace? Throw it overboard and sail off to a new life? One thing for sure: I knew I'd never see her again, and I'd live to regret it.

※

That's where the recording ended. And, I was pretty sure, the story as well. The thought that I would no longer dream in black and white, no longer dream of Adeline, was overwhelmingly depressing to me.

VII

I went back to the life I'd known before Adeline, Larry, or Sharon came into my life. I had no regrets. I'd had one last unexpected hurrah. One brief flash of excitement and mystery before I took that inevitable slide down, down, down, to that last pathetic wheeze, that final whimper we all have to look forward to.

As before, I slept as late as possible and dreamed vividly —in color—mostly about times gone by. I was always young in my dreams, and so were the other characters, be they people I had once known or complete strangers. I got up, did my exercise routine, ate my cereal with blueberries, tried to do a little writing, tried to read as many great books as possible, watched the old movies even though I'd seen all the good ones dozens of times, and every day I took my bike ride.

Every day the same circuit: up the hill on 16th Street, west on Idaho, north on Ocean Ave., and then east on San Vicente. I would take San Vicente to 26th Street, turn right, and go south to California (my street), then west back home.

It must have been four or five days after the last dream. I was stopped at the intersection of San Vicente and 7th. It was a Saturday, and there were a lot of people out jogging and cycling. I chanced to look to my right while waiting for the interminable series of traffic light changes: green for southbound but not for northbound, green for northbound, but not for southbound. Left turn arrows for all four directions. Then, finally, a green light for me, going east. That's when I caught a glimpse of her. She was a beautiful blond, no more than twenty-one, wearing a red jogging suit with white piping, straight hair pulled back into a ponytail, and sunglasses.

And she was a dead ringer for Adeline. If Adeline lived in my time, this is how she would look. For a split second our eyes met, even though we were both wearing shades. And she smiled. Right at me. Even at my best, I'm no bargain to look at. But, in my cycling helmet, black kung-fu pants, blue-and-white three-quarter-sleeve T-shirt commemorating Creedence Clearwater Revival's fortieth anniversary, and the black-and-white low-top sneakers that resembled the ones I wore when I was ten, I looked especially dorky. And yet, she smiled at me. The light turned green and I cycled on, certain I had imagined the whole thing. She was, no doubt, smiling at the young man on the bike beside me.

But then, the next day. Same corner. There she was again. This time I stopped and lowered my shades. I looked right at her. She smiled that smile that always dazzled me and lowered her shades. Our eyes locked. It *was* Adeline.

She crossed against the light to the southeast corner of 7th and San Vicente. On it stood a house that was at least eighty years old, a white wooden craftsman-style with the classic California overlapping peaked roofs. Against that backdrop, she shed her red jogging gear. It turned into a black-and-white, forties-style frock with a short, tailored summer jacket over it, and a simple broad-brimmed hat that dipped over one eye. Her hair was sculpted in permanent waves, just as it had been in my dream. She beckoned to me. I didn't hesitate. I started across 7th, paying no attention to the redness of the light.

An oncoming SUV, in a hurry to get through the intersection before the light changed, broadsided me without even slowing down. The bike and I flew halfway across San Vicente. A crowd gathered and sirens approached. I felt no pain, just an incredible peace — and joy. Joy because I could still see her standing there in front of the big white house. But it looked a bit different. It didn't have the fancy brick gateway from a few moments earlier. She smiled and waved, and out of the crumpled heap of broken bones and bloody clothing of the old man lying lifeless in the street, rose me, Larry Holden. I was dressed in my usual trench coat and gray fedora. I walked across the street to her.

The crowd had disappeared. There was hardly any traffic. San Vicente had become a narrow, two-lane road. And it was all in black and white. She took my hand, and we walked through the gate of what I now knew was to be our house. Her Delahaye was all fixed up and parked in the garage. She looked up at me. We kissed. She asked me if I had forgiven her. I didn't know what she was talking about.

After twenty years trembling on the brink of rock stardom and fifteen years working at record companies, Ted Myers left the music business—or perhaps it was the other way around—and took a job as a copywriter at an advertising agency. This cemented his determination to make his mark as an author.

As a musician, Ted sang, played guitar, and wrote songs for five seminal rock bands between 1964 and 1984. Perhaps the most noteworthy of these was his first, The Lost, based in Boston, MA, signed to Capitol Records in 1965. In 1967 Ted started Chamaeleon Church (with Chevy Chase on drums!), and in the '70s, two more bands in California. But, ironically, the most well-known band he played with was Ultimate Spinach, a San Francisco-style Boston band that was founded in 1967. In 1972 he wrote the song "Going in Circles" for the major motion picture *X, Y & Zee* starring Elizabeth Taylor and Michael Caine. It was recorded by Three Dog Night, selling about 6 million records. As a compilation producer for Rhino Records, his folk box set *Washington Square Memoirs* earned a Grammy nomination in 2001.

His short fiction has appeared in many literary magazines and anthologies. His epic and amusing memoir, *Making It: Music, Sex & Drugs in the Golden Age of Rock* was published in 2017. *Fluffy's Revolution* (2019) was his first novel. His second novel, *Paris Escapade*, was published in December 2020.

Ted lives alone in Santa Monica, California, as a happy recluse.

Made in the USA
Columbia, SC
09 August 2023